THE FORTUNES OF TEXAS

Follow the lives and loves of a complex family with a rich history and deep ties in the Lone Star State

FORTUNE'S FAMILY SCANDAL

With Archibald Fortune's death comes the revelation of a stunning secret: The Emerald Ridge scion had three separate families and one child he'd always longed to find! Can his shocked children come together to find Archibald's missing heir and claim the family inheritance—or will strife tear them apart?

FORTUNE'S BUNDLE OF JOY

Shelby Fortune's about to make the ultimate pivot...from pageant queen to single mom. With her life upturned due to the betrayal of a father she clearly never knew, the last thing on her mind is love. But she might be powerless against the elusive Cameron Waite...a man as resistant to romance as she is!

Dear Reader,

It's always fun visiting with the Fortunes of Texas and seeing what they're up to. And in this book, they're up to a lot.

Shelby Fortune is sweet, funny and upbeat, even when her whole world is crashing down around her. Which isn't easy when your career is heading downhill fast, you've discovered a devastating family secret, you're four months pregnant by a guy who's skipped town, and you don't know how to tell anyone. Well, okay, except for the handsome stranger you just met as you were passing out on the sidewalk.

I hate when that happens.

Cameron Waite has no idea what to make of Shelby when she literally falls into his arms. Except that she's pretty daggone sweet. And funny. And upbeat. All things he hasn't felt himself for some time. It's impossible for him to not get drawn into all the goings-on in her life. And wow, there's a lot going on there.

Then again, he hasn't exactly had an uneventful year himself, what with discovering a long-lost twin brother he never knew he had, realizing the career choice he made may not have been the best one for him, being jilted by an ex-fiancée who turned out to be anything but sweet, funny and upbeat, and—

Well, let's just say Shelby and Cameron both have a lot to sort out in their lives right now. Good thing they have each other. Or will. Eventually...

I had such a good time writing about Shelby and Cameron. I hope you enjoy reading about them just as much.

All the best,

Elizabeth

FORTUNE'S BUNDLE OF JOY

ELIZABETH BEVARLY

THE FORTUNES OF TEXAS

Special thanks and acknowledgment are given to Elizabeth Bevarly for her contribution to The Fortunes of Texas: Fortune's Family Secrets miniseries.

Recycling programs for this product may not exist in your area.

ISBN-13: 978-1-335-14331-0

Fortune's Bundle of Joy

For questions and comments about the quality of this book, please contact us at CustomerService@Harlequin.com.

Harlequin Enterprises ULC
22 Adelaide St. West, 41st Floor
Toronto, Ontario M5H 4E3, Canada
www.Harlequin.com

HarperCollins Publishers
Macken House, 39/40 Mayor Street Upper,
Dublin 1, D01 C9W8, Ireland
www.HarperCollins.com

Printed in Lithuania

Elizabeth Bevarly is the *New York Times* and *USA TODAY* bestselling author of more than eighty books. She has called home such exotic places as Puerto Rico and New Jersey but now lives outside her hometown of Louisville, Kentucky, with her husband and cat. When she's not writing or reading, she enjoys cooking, tending her kitchen garden and feeding the local wildlife. Visit her at elizabethbevarly.com for news and lots of fun stuff.

Books by Elizabeth Bevarly

The Fortunes of Texas: Fortune's Hidden Treasure

His Family Fortune

The Fortunes of Texas: Fortune's Secret Children

Nine Months to a Fortune

The Fortunes of Texas: Fortune's Family Secrets

Fortune's Bundle of Joy

Harlequin Special Edition

Seasons in Sudbury

Heir in a Year
Her Second-Chance Family
Keeping Her Secret

Lucky Stars

Be Careful What You Wish For
Her Good-Luck Charm
Secret under the Stars

Visit the Author Profile page
at Harlequin.com for more titles.

For Susan Litman,
with a million thank yous for
bringing me into the Fortune family.

Chapter One

Shelby Fortune had a to-do list that was a mile long, and by noon she'd barely made her way through ten feet of it. It was just such a balmy, beautiful day in Emerald Ridge, Texas, and those didn't come often in early February. Although she'd managed to complete a few tasks—she'd picked up necessities at ER Grocery, mailed a birthday card to a high school friend, returned some library books and dropped off a couple of pageant gowns at the dry cleaner—every time she exited an establishment, she just wanted to dawdle on her way to the next, loving the feel of the sunshine pouring over her.

After snagging a parking spot just off Emerald Ridge Boulevard, the main drag of downtown, she looked at the list she'd tossed into the passenger seat after striking through each item completed. She frowned. Dang it. *Eat breakfast* was still at the top without a line crossed through it. She'd totally forgotten to eat, due in no small part to the decaf maple latte with which she'd started the day. Her stomach rumbled. It had definitely worn off. But she didn't have time for lunch—which was a few more items down the list, anyway, thanks to her dilly-dallying—because the one item she absolutely could not miss was fifteen minutes away. An appointment with her

OB/GYN. Grabbing a bite would have to wait, because today, she was going to find out the gender of her baby!

Which was possibly contributing to why she wasn't getting as much done as she should. Her brain was scrambled from weeks of seesawing over whether or not she wanted to find out in advance or be surprised on the day of delivery. Then again, one thing she'd learned over the last few months was that the simple act of being pregnant went a long way toward the scrambling of a person's brain. In a word, *Oof.*

She experienced a momentary pang of regret that her baby's father wouldn't be here to make the discovery with her. Then she remembered her ex-boyfriend, Dylan, was a lowdown dirty dog who wanted nothing to do with either one of them. They were both better off without him.

Downtown was bustling at the weekday lunch hour, and Shelby had had to park two blocks away from the office building where her doctor was located. Not a problem, though. She was a champion walker after two decades of training for—and winning—dozens of beauty pageants. She smiled at the passersby she encountered and inhaled the luscious aromas of lunchtime floating from the cafés she strode by. The tidy limestone storefronts glittered in the sunlight, a soft breeze danced with her blond hair and flowered sundress, and bursts of twangy country and lively Tejano music peppered the air from passing cars.

She and her younger-by-a-year sister, Jillian, had spent their middle and high school years at an elite boarding school just outside Philadelphia, then attended colleges out of state, and Shelby loved being able to call Emerald Ridge home full-time now. Their father, Archibald Fortune, had wanted them to have a better, broader life than he'd had himself growing up here—before he'd made billions with his airline—but she'd never felt suited to big-city living in the North. Shelby was a Texas girl through and through and never wanted to leave again.

As she waited at the final crosswalk for the signal to change, she suddenly felt a little lightheaded. She placed a hand against the lamppost to steady herself, and by the time the chime rang to say it was safe to cross, she was feeling better. She took her time, though, as she made her way to the other side of the street, wishing belatedly that she'd worn something a little more practical than kitten-heeled pumps for her errands. Then again, these were pretty much the most practical shoes she owned. Another byproduct of her years on the circuit.

Note to self, Shelby. Add Buy some flats *to your next to-do list.* Her days of competing were numbered anyway with her impending motherhood, especially after the disastrous pageant she'd entered—and had *not* won—last week.

Try as she might to push thoughts of that debacle away, the memories came crashing back. She'd assumed she would easily make the top five in the inaugural Miss Texas Incandescence pageant. That wasn't ego talking, it was a simple matter of fact. Shelby Fortune had always made it to the top five in any pageant she entered—from Little Miss Watermelon Festival to Miss America. She was a Texas legend when it came to pageants. Again, just fact. And considering the newness of the Miss US Incandescence franchise, it had been reasonable to assume they would want as many recognizable names in the finals as they could get, to help launch it both locally and nationally. But she hadn't even made the top *ten.*

What had been truly jarring was the judging for the evening gowns, when the panel members had taken to frankly commenting on every contestant's physical appearance. It was something that had never happened in pageants before, but which the contestants discovered, on the spot, would be a defining feature of Miss US Incandescence, to both set it apart from other competitions and "capture the current American fascination with frank speaking." In other words, a gimmick, as far as Shelby was concerned. And when the judges had gotten to her…

Well. Supposedly polite-sounding phrases like *full hips* and *rounded tummy* and *recent thirtieth birthday* had sounded anything *but* polite. And the judges' expressions when delivering them had been nothing short of distasteful. Suddenly, all those years of defending the pageant world as being about so much more than an assessment of physical beauty—because, to Shelby, competing had always seemed more akin to being a professional athlete—had felt like a slap in the face.

Whoa. As Shelby drew nearer to her doctor's building, her head began to swim again. She stopped, inhaled a few deep breaths, then moved forward, taking her steps more deliberately. She thought she was doing okay, but when she gripped the door handle and began to pull it toward herself, moving back to let it swing in front of her, her body somehow just kept going, even though her feet had stopped. The next thing she knew, the sky was spinning above her, and she was tipping backward. Fear seized her when she realized she had no idea which way was up, and it vaguely occurred to her that the next item on her to-do list was going to be an ambulance ride to the ER.

Then, miraculously, from somewhere beside her, a

strong arm roped around her waist, pulling her back to her feet and steadying her. No—*more* than that. Someone was actually lifting her off the sidewalk and moving her away from the door, then setting her down again along the wall beside it. And he was murmuring something about *Easy does it* in a way that made a shudder of something warm and wistful—and in no way easy—wind its way through her.

Instinctively, Shelby opened one hand over the cool limestone to help her get her bearings, then covered the arm still curled around her waist with the other. After a moment, when the world stopped spinning, she turned her head to see who had saved her from becoming a heap on the sidewalk. And, suddenly, the world went all cattywampus again. Only this time, it wasn't because her brain was fritzing from too little food and too much sugar. This time it was because she was looking into the most gorgeous blue eyes she'd ever seen.

"Are you okay?" those eyes asked.

Oh, no, wait. It wasn't the *eyes* asking. It was the man they were attached to. Who was even more gorgeous than they were. Under a chocolate brown Stetson, dark blond hair framed a face that was all strong lines and chiseled features, from the elegant cheekbones to the narrow nose to the square chin to the kind of mouth that made a woman think about things she had no business thinking about on a busy street in the middle of the day. Even after he released Shelby and she regained her composure, he towered over her—no easy feat, since she stood five-ten herself without the heels—and the sunlight behind him gave him an aura of otherworldliness more suited to a caped superhero. But instead of a cape, he was dressed in dark jeans and a camel-colored blazer and a crisp white shirt that was open at the neck. His boots were hand-tooled leather the same color as his Stetson. And he still looked very concerned.

He knew she was okay, though, right? She had replied to his question, hadn't she? When she saw that he was still looking at her expectantly, she realized that no, she hadn't. Probably because all the words got dried up in her mouth the minute she got a good look at him.

"I'm fine," she finally managed.

He didn't look convinced. Those blue, blue eyes were still full of genuine concern. "You sure?"

She nodded, not trusting herself to not blurt out that he was the most mesmerizing man she'd ever seen. Then she released the wall to make her way into the building… only to wobble once more and return her hand to the cool stone. The kind stranger reached out again to help her, but she held up her free hand, palm out, in a silent bid to stop him.

"I'm fine," she insisted. "I just need a minute. I shouldn't have skipped breakfast."

"I don't see how anyone can skip breakfast," he said. "If I don't have the rancher's special from Cameron's Kitchen every morning, I can't function for the rest of the day."

Shelby was more than a little familiar with all the eating establishments in town, but she'd never heard of Cameron's Kitchen. Nor could she think of a single place that offered anything called a rancher's special.

"Cameron's Kitchen," she repeated. "That either has to be a brand-spanking-new place here in Emerald Ridge or you're from out of town."

He smiled. And, *whoosh*, there went her equilibrium again. "A little of both," he said.

He stuck out his hand, but this time, it was clearly just for a shake. Automatically, Shelby took it, and he gave hers a single, confident pump before releasing it. A sizzle of heat wound up her arm at the brief contact, and she felt oddly bereft when he let go.

"I'm Cameron," he said. "Cameron Waite. I've only been living in Emerald Ridge for about a month. And I make the rancher's special in my own kitchen. Bacon, eggs, biscuits, gravy, the whole shebang."

Shelby shook her head. How could he eat that every morning and look as fit and healthy as he did?

As if reading her mind, he smiled and added, "I eat pretty clean otherwise."

She nodded. "Gotcha. So you're a rancher, then?"

Kind of odd to ask him that, because she knew the only ranches in Emerald Ridge were the Fortune's Gold Guest Ranch and Spa—which was actually a sprawling resort that brought visitors from all over the country—and the Fortune and Daughters Ranch, where Shelby lived with her parents and sister. And it wasn't a real working ranch, either, though her father did collect rare horses, more than a dozen of which had free rein of the place.

"Nah," he told her. "That's just what I always ate for breakfast growing up, and that's what my mom called it, since she grew up on a ranch. She always insisted a growing boy needed a lot of protein to start the day."

Shelby's stomach growled at the talk of food, and they both chuckled. Cameron Waite reached for the door again and opened it. "Come on," he said, sweeping a hand in that direction. "There's a snack bar in the lobby. Wherever you're headed can wait a few minutes while I grab you something to eat."

"You don't have to do that," she protested. "I can—"

"I insist," he said. "My parents brought me up to do a good deed every day, and I'm already halfway through this one not having done a single one. Let me get you a granola bar or something."

"Thank you. That's very kind of you."

She supposed there had been a time in her yearlong relationship with Dylan when he had offered to do something like that for her, but she sure couldn't recall when it might have been. Now some hot guy she'd only known a matter of minutes was taking the time out of his day to make sure a stranger had something to eat.

As she preceded him into the lobby, Cameron removed his Stetson again—wow, his parents really had brought him up right—then he guided her to a bench and made his way to a kiosk in the corner. By the time he returned with a bag of pretzels and a bottle of water, she was almost feeling herself again. She thanked him, thinking he would then be on his way, but he took a seat beside her instead.

"I was gonna get you some pistachios since protein is usually good in a situation like this, but then I was worried you might have a nut allergy. Pretzels are usually pretty safe. These are gluten-free," he added with another one of those gorgeous smiles. "Just in case."

Who was this man who seemed to think of everything? Shelby wondered. He was straight out of a Hallmark movie.

She laughed. "Okay, you're not a rancher, but…maybe a nutritionist?"

He chuckled, too. "No. I work for my family's business. I'm a banker."

Shelby couldn't hide her surprise. "I never would have guessed that in a million years. You don't look like a banker."

"Yeah, well, sometimes I don't feel like one, either. It's not exactly in my genes. But I'm the CEO of Waite Financial, headquartered in Dallas." She was about to ask him what brought him to Emerald Ridge, but he quickly added, "And you are?"

It was only then that she realized she'd never introduced herself. Holy smoke, she really was out of it today. She opened the bag of pretzels as she replied, "I'm Shelby Fortune."

His eyebrows shot up at her introduction. "You're one of the Fortunes?"

She nodded as she munched and swallowed a pretzel, not surprised by his recognition of her name. Everyone who came to Emerald Ridge heard about the Fortunes, often within minutes of arriving in town. It wasn't unusual for them to *meet* a Fortune within minutes of arriving in town. The place was crawling with them. There were several branches of the family either from here or recently arrived here, many of whom Shelby herself hadn't met, despite the fact that they were cousins. Distant cousins in some cases, but cousins nonetheless.

"Yep," she told him. "I'm one of Archibald Fortune's girls. He's the CEO of Fortune Air? I have a sister named Jillian, and my mama is Agatha Fortune."

"I fly Fortune Air a lot, but I don't think I've heard of anybody else in your family," Cameron said after a minute. "But that would explain why you didn't recognize me."

"Why would I recognize you? You're not a Fortune."

"No, but my twin brother is, and I look just like him so I get mistaken for him a lot around here. He's Drake Fortune."

"Nope, never met him. But how could you have a twin brother who's a Fortune and not be one yourself?"

He expelled a restless breath. "That is a long story. But in a nutshell, he and I were both put up for adoption as infants. He was adopted by one family here in Emerald Ridge, and I was adopted by another family in Dallas. We never knew about each other until last summer. Surely, you heard about the Courtney Wellington thing."

Oh, jeez, who *hadn't* heard about that? It had been the most major event in Emerald Ridge's history, filled with all sorts of scandals. Everything from black-market babies to arson and murder.

"Y'all were two of the Texas Royale Adoption babies," Shelby guessed.

Cameron nodded. "Yeah. Separated within days of our birth."

"Wow. I mean, I'd heard that that happened, of course, but it's so hard to imagine. I can't believe how many lives that awful woman wrecked. I'm glad you and your brother were able to find each other."

Cameron nodded. "It was wild when we finally made contact as adults, each of us a mirror image of the other but never having met. It's been great, though," he hurried to add. "I never had any siblings growing up, and Drake and I hit it off immediately. His parents, Darla and Hayden, have made me feel like a member of their family, which has been really nice now that my own folks are gone. They even said if they'd known Drake had a brother, they would have adopted both of us. Then again, I can't imagine not ever knowing my mom and dad. They were wonderful people."

Shelby smiled. "So you're basically a Fortune with a different name and family. Kind of had the best of two worlds."

He smiled back. "Yeah. Our birth mother was born here in Emerald Ridge, too, but she came from a pretty poor family, and her folks didn't do right by her when she told them about her condition. She didn't have much choice other than to put us up for adoption. But I sincerely doubt she thought we'd be separated, and… And I have no idea why I'm telling you all this," he finished suddenly. "I'm sorry. Guess you're just one of those people who's really easy to talk to."

Shelby didn't have any idea why he was sharing his life story with her, either. But she was weirdly happy that he was. It had been a long time since she'd had a conversation like this, with someone new, learning fascinating things about them. And Cameron Waite was as easy to talk to as he was to look at. But if she didn't hurry, she was going to be late for her ultrasound.

"I'm glad you did," she said. "I'd actually love to sit here and talk all day, but I'm gonna miss my doctor's appointment if I do. So as much as I hate to, I need to get going." She started to stand, but was immediately swamped by another wave of dizziness, so sat down again. "In a minute," she added.

Cameron took the bottle of water from her and unscrewed the top, then handed it back. "Have another pretzel. Drink some water. And let me give you a hand. What floor do you need to go to?"

"Three," she said. She did as he suggested and enjoyed another pretzel and a swallow of water.

"I just came from up there myself. Which doctor?"

"Elena Chavez," Shelby replied after another sip.

"I just came from there, too."

She almost choked on her water, then laughed. "What were you doing at a gynecologist's office?"

"That's another long story," he said. "But come on. I'll make sure you don't stumble along the way."

Somehow Shelby refrained from commenting on that. She felt like she'd been stumbling along the way ever since discovering she was going to have a baby. This after having spent her entire life planning everything down to the last detail. She knew there were plenty of people out there who just kind of floated through life, taking one thing at a time, enjoying every moment *in* the moment. Folks who never knew what was coming next but looked forward to discovering whatever surprise life dropped into their lap. Shelby was *not* one of those people. Even as a child, she'd awoken in the morning and planned out her day, listing all the things she wanted to get accomplished and then doing them. As she'd grown older, she'd started scheduling her whole week. Then her whole month. As an adult, she spent every New Year's Day orchestrating the entire year ahead.

Of course, she hadn't exactly planned on getting pregnant. Or on discovering that Dylan would turn out to be such a massive jerk. But once the shock of both had worn off, Shelby had gone right back to her planning and list making again. And this time, she was going to stick to both. Item number one on that list: *Never trust a man to do the right thing.*

She looked at Cameron Waite again, and her conviction on that began to waver. Even after only talking to him so briefly, he seemed like a really good guy. Then again, so had Dylan when she met him. People always presented their best face when they were meeting someone for the first time. Sure, Cameron was being chivalrous right now, helping a woman in distress. Who knew what really lay beneath the kind—and gorgeous—exterior? She would be well served to just stick with her plans, and lists, for the foreseeable future.

After all, her good organizational skills was just one reason she'd done so well competing in pageants for so many years. Preparation was key in that environment, and Shelby Fortune was its queen. When she first started, the age limit for contestants in most pageants was the late twenties, so she'd planned to retire at twenty-eight and start her own coaching business, helping other girls find the confidence, character and camaraderie she'd found herself while competing. But the age limit was lifted a while back, so she'd decided to keep on keeping on. She'd liked competing. She'd always felt like she learned something new about herself with every pageant experience she had. In hindsight, though, she should absolutely have stuck to her original plan. What happened last week hadn't been just a surprise. It had been a shock to her system, one that ensured she'd never set foot on a pageant stage again. She was even thinking of changing her focus once she did start coaching others, putting emphasis on things like, oh, she didn't know, *character* and *integrity* instead of poise and interview questions, and who did some judges think they were, judging people like that, and…

Um…where was she? Anyway, surprises these days were *not* her friend.

Then again, she thought as Cameron helped her to standing, hooking her arm loosely through his, there were some surprises that, even if she couldn't quite trust them, still made for a nice way to spend an afternoon.

By the time the elevator reached the third floor, Cameron Waite noticed that his pretty new friend had finished her pretzels and downed the last of her water. With Shelby Fortune's arm still linked through his, he steered them both into the hall, and she tossed the remnants of her snack into a bin along the way. Even though she'd indicated earlier that she was about to be late for her appointment, she didn't seem to be in any hurry to reach her destination at the end of the hall. Although she no longer seemed wobbly, the arm looped through his snugged a little tighter, and she slowed her pace, then came to a complete halt a few feet shy of the door.

"Well, I guess this is my stop," she said, her voice sounding as uncertain as the rest of her seemed to be, her hazel eyes—a beautiful mix of green and brown—filled with unmistakable apprehension. "Thanks for the escort. And the pretzels," she added with a smile.

But her smile this time wasn't as cheerful as her other ones had been. There was something in this one that was almost fearful.

"Feeling dizzy again?" he said gently. Mostly because he didn't want to ask her if she was afraid of something, since that seemed a little invasive. Even though she suddenly did seem to be fearful of something.

She shook her head. "No, my snack did the trick. Thanks again."

But she didn't release his arm, nor did she advance a single step toward the doctor's office door. Cameron was certainly no expert on women's health, but he knew regular visits like this were a normal part of life for the opposite sex.

It did seem strange that she'd stopped outside the door, looking afraid to go in. But she didn't ask him to stick around, either.

So he said, "Well, then, I guess I'll see you out and about in Emerald Ridge, Shelby Fortune."

Instead of saying something about how she was looking forward to it—because, to be honest, he really would kind of like to see her again—she blurted, "I'm just suddenly kind of nervous is all."

Made sense.

Then she further blurted, "I'm having a pretty major ultrasound today."

His eyebrows shot up at that, and, unable to help himself, he dropped his gaze to her abdomen just as she opened her free hand over her dress. It was one of those long, flowy ones, spattered with little blue flowers, and now that she was pressing the fabric over her midsection, he could detect just a hint of a baby bump there.

"You're pregnant?" he asked. Immediately, he shook his head. "I mean, of course you're pregnant if you're getting an ultrasound in an OB/GYN's office."

"Yep," she told him with a shaky sigh. "Eighteen

weeks. I'm due June fifth. But I haven't told anyone yet. Well, except you. And, of course, my baby's father."

He felt both strangely honored and kind of concerned about the revelation. She'd mentioned earlier her folks and sister. A woman as outgoing and chatty as she was must have a slew of friends, too. Why hadn't she told any of them yet… and had instead chosen to confide in a virtual stranger?

The question must have shown on his face, because she continued, "I wanted to tell my family, but the timing was never right. Daddy travels a lot, and my sister's been involved with a project at the children's hospital and spending a lot of time volunteering there. Then I just figured I'd wait until I know everything is okay with the baby and moving along on schedule. Today Dr. Chavez is doing what's called an anatomy scan. They're going to be able to find out all kinds of stuff about whether my baby is healthy." Her expression grew more concerned. "Or not. I mean, the chances that there's anything wrong are slim, but…"

"But there's still a chance," he finished for her.

She nodded silently, looking even more fearful. It was such a change from the smiling, bubbly, funny woman he'd met downstairs. Her anxiety was almost palpable. He'd be worried about stuff, too, if he was having a baby. No wonder she didn't want to go in alone.

"I'll wait with you until your husband gets here," he offered.

Now a flash of annoyance crossed her face. "Yeah, well, you're gonna have a long wait." She lifted her left hand for his inspection. Although she wore several rings, the one on her ring finger was way too big and ornate to be a wedding or engagement ring. "Dylan wasn't my husband, and he hightailed it to Austin a couple weeks ago when he realized that being a father was going to cramp his style of being the world's greatest tech bro." She dropped her hand to her side again, but she didn't stop talking. "And he made it abundantly clear that he's not coming back. He reminded me how, when we first got together, he told me there was no way he would ever want to have kids. But that was okay, because I didn't think I wanted them, either, at that point. It just sort of happened, you know?"

She drew a deep, quavering breath, but before he could get a word in, she pressed on. "Of course, it didn't take long for me to be really happy about it. I thought over time he'd be happy, too, but *nooo*. On his way out the door, he promised to send a check for 'the baby'—not 'my baby' or even 'your baby,' just '*the baby*,' as if it just appeared in my womb out of nowhere—every month. To which I replied, 'You're damned right you will.' I mean, I'm fine financially, but I figure it's never too early to start a college fund, and jeez, he's half responsible. Of course, every now and then I wonder if I should try harder to make him a part of my baby's life, even if he is a contemptible pig. And now everyone in Emerald Ridge knows we broke up, so once I *do* start telling people I'm pregnant, it's gonna be a bit of a shock, you know? 'Oh my gracious goodness, that scion of respectability Shelby Fortune is carrying a baby out of wedlock, oh let me just clutch my pearls.' Like do people even still use the term *out of wedlock*? Oh, yeah. Here in Texas, they do. I'm never going to hear the end of it after—"

She stopped abruptly, looking horrified by all that

she'd revealed. She even lifted her hand to clamp it over her mouth, then closed her eyes in embarrassment. She lifted her hand long enough to say, "Oh, my God. I am so sorry. I can't believe I just dumped all that into your lap. Now who's the one saying stuff they can't explain?" Then put it right back over her mouth again as if fearful she'd do it again.

Cameron bit back a smile. If he'd had any doubts about Shelby's well-being, they were gone. Yeah, she was a little fearful and anxious—who wouldn't be in her situation?—but she was gonna be just fine.

All he said in response to her long diatribe, though, was, "Dylan sounds like a fool-headed numbskull to me."

She laughed lightly at his remark, then dropped her hand again, and some of her earlier spark seemed to return. "You're a lot more polite in your name-calling than I've been," she said with a smile that was considerably less tense. She finally removed her arm from his, straightened upright and blew out another shaky breath. "Okay, Shelby, you've got this," she told herself. To Cameron, she added, "I'm gonna be fine. My baby's gonna be fine. Everything is gonna be fine."

She *almost* sounded like she believed that. And maybe a part of her did. But it never hurt to have a little extra support in a tough situation. So he told her, "Look, let me go in with you." When she opened her mouth to object, he hurried on, "Just till you get called back. I'm still working on that good deed. Anybody can do pretzels and water."

She looked like she was going to protest again, then her expression turned grateful. "Thank you," she murmured. "I appreciate it. But once they call me back, I insist you get on with your day. I'm sure you have a million things to do besides hold the hand of a scared pregnant woman."

Actually, Cameron only had a couple thousand things to do today. But not a single one of them was more appealing than holding Shelby Fortune's hand. Looping her arm back through his, he moved them both forward, reached for the door handle and escorted her inside.

Chapter Two

As always, the waiting room was packed, Shelby noticed upon entering and signing in for her appointment with Dr. Chavez. And, as always, nearly everyone with a baby bump had their partners with them. She even recognized a lot of them. Including Brittany Carew-Meyer and her wife, Amber, who owned Shelby's favorite boutique in town and were expecting their second child. They both lifted a hand in greeting when they saw her, but their expressions turned inquisitive when she and Cameron sat down together, as if to say, *Wait, who's this guy? This guy's* not *Dylan.* Shelby only smiled back and silently willed them be patient until she could explain in an atmosphere that wasn't a room full of people just dying to hear the latest gossip.

Still, it was a little unsettling for her to realize—again—that she would be going into parenthood without a partner. Not that Dylan had come to any of her other doctor visits, but she'd always known she could fill him in with the details after she got home, since he worked remotely. Well, sometimes she could tell him the details when she got home, since he seemed to choose her doctor visit days to work from the Coffee Connection instead of home.

All right, all right, so Dylan hadn't exactly been World's Greatest Dad material even before he bugged out to Austin. She probably should have realized from the get-go that their baby would create waves in their relationship that were nothing short of tsunamic. Even so, better to learn that before her little bambino was born than have him dump both of them while she was still adjusting to some major life changes.

How was she supposed to tell everyone she was pregnant? Especially her family? She knew her parents weren't going to approve right off the bat—they were both super traditional and conservative when it came to family matters. But there wasn't a doubt in her mind that they would eventually be delighted by the arrival of their first grandchild. Her sister, Jillian, would likewise be over the moon about having a new niece or nephew running around the ranch, since that would make her the *hella cool auntie.* Especially if said niece or nephew got the Fortune horse gene, which Jillian had in spades but had somehow bypassed Shelby.

"Looks like it's still a full house today," Cameron said from beside her.

"It's always like this," she told him. "Not just patients for annual stuff, either. There have been lots of new babies showing up in Emerald Ridge lately. A fair number of them Fortunes, now that I think about it."

"And now you're going to have another one."

Another ribbon of apprehension rippled through her. She was 99.999 percent sure that her baby was healthy and growing just fine. But until she got official reassurance from Dr. Chavez, her concerns weren't going to go away. Probably even after she knew all was well, her worries would linger until she held the little bundle in her arms and could count all the fingers and toes herself. A part of Shelby was starting to suspect that fear for her child's safety and well-being would be a constant companion for the rest of her life.

"Yep," she said, hoping none of that trepidation showed. "I don't think I'll ever have to worry about there not being enough kids to invite to any future birthday parties."

"Well, I hope you send me an invitation, too."

Shelby glanced over at his comment and found Cameron looking as surprised by it as she was.

"I mean, if you want to," he hurried on. "And if I'm still in town and all by then."

Even having known him such a short time, she kinda did find herself wanting to invite Cameron to any future birthdays her child would celebrate. He already had a tie to the little Fortune-to-be that no one else had—he knew about her baby and, more to the point, cared about her baby. Even so, it was the second part of his comment that caught her attention more.

"You're not going to be staying in Emerald Ridge?"

She didn't know why the news of his in-no-way-imminent departure bothered her. She'd just met the man, for heaven's sake. Somehow, though, the idea that he might not always be around didn't sit well with her.

"I don't know," he said, suddenly seeming a little uncomfortable. "I bought a place here in Emerald Ridge a month ago to be closer to a project I'm headquartering here. Depending on how that goes, I may move myself more here, or I may go back to Dallas full-time."

She was about to ask him about his project, but he kept talking before she had a chance.

"It's been great getting closer to Drake—I will say that. But the biggest chunk of my life is still in Dallas. I've been driving back and forth a lot since discovering I had a twin brother, and that's getting old. But I do like it here. A lot. And Drake's the only family I have now, so..."

He didn't finish the sentence. Then again, he didn't have to. Just the way he said it made it clear he thought family was important. But there was something in his voice, too, that made her think he wasn't quite sure who or where his family truly was. Was it in Dallas, where he grew up with his parents, or here in Emerald Ridge with his newly discovered brother? Emerald Ridge was his birthplace, as he'd said, even if he didn't remember that part. It had to be strange, discovering so late in life that your entire existence could have taken a completely different track, and you could have ended up someplace else altogether. Maybe neither Dallas nor Emerald Ridge felt like home to him. Maybe he felt kind of lost.

Shelby sympathized. Her parents had sent her and Jillian off to live another life for the better part of the year when they were barely out of grade school, so that the sisters would have a deeper understanding of the big, wide world out there and more opportunities than either of them had growing up here in Emerald Ridge. In a way, though, living away from home for all that time had only reinforced Shelby's realization that Emerald Ridge was exactly where she belonged.

Though the family part, she got.

Due to spending so much time away when she was young, and thanks to her father's incessant business traveling, Shelby didn't feel much of a family connection to her own flesh and blood, either, other than Jillian. And even there, she and her sister had both done their own thing for years. As they grew to adulthood, they both became involved in totally different pursuits. They were close, sure, but they really didn't spend as much time together these days as they used to.

It didn't sound like Cameron, though, had had a chance like Shelby had to explore where he belonged. At least not until recently. Something like that could take a long time to figure out. Even after all these years, Shelby had days where she felt adrift. Now more than ever with the prospect of motherhood ahead. Which had her wondering if anyone ever really found their place in the world.

"Well, if you stay in Emerald Ridge," she told Cameron, "you will absolutely get a birthday invitation every June."

His clouded expression cleared some at that. But he didn't seem to relax entirely. "Thanks."

One of the medical assistants came out to call a name that Shelby remembered as being several above her own when she signed in. Depending on which doctor that person was seeing, it could be a while before her own name was called. Might as well get comfortable. She toed off both shoes—they'd started feeling tight over the last couple of weeks—and looked at Cameron again.

"So you never told me what you were doing in Dr. Chavez's office earlier," she said. "Whatever the reason, it has to be interesting. The only time men ever brave entry into a place like this is if they're about to become a parent, too. So fess, up, Cameron Waite. Is there a woman out there with a little baby Waite-ing in the wings?"

She arched a brow in a way she hoped was comically suspicious at her not-so-clever pun. But, wow, did she miss the mark. Because the look that came over his face just then was…

Shelby had, of course, heard the expression *Like a deer in the headlights* many times. But she didn't think she'd ever really appreciated exactly what it meant until that moment. Because Cameron was suddenly looking at her like she was bearing down on him in a semi. Filled with cement. Doing ninety. At night. On an icy road.

As quickly as the expression overcame him, however, it eased. Somewhat. There was still a little panic in his eyes, but the mouth that had been set in a tight line eased, and the almost palpable dread lessened. Shelby had never wanted to ask someone what was wrong more than she did with Cameron in that moment. But she somehow sensed that doing so would be in no way welcome.

Finally, he grinned in a way that wasn't quite happy and laughed in a way that wasn't quite funny. Then he lifted a hand, palm outward, as if he were about to swear an oath. "I assure you, Shelby Fortune, that I am *not* a man who's looking to walk down a path toward fatherhood anytime soon. Maybe not ever."

He spoke with so much conviction when he said the *not ever* part that she almost believed him. But there was something else in his voice that made her think he wished he felt otherwise.

She did her best to smile. "Well, you don't have to make it sound like it's number eight million and thirty-seven on your to-do list," she told him. "Right after wrestling an alligator and drinking hemlock."

He laughed again, and this time, there was something

a little more natural in the sound. Whatever that strange, anxious moment was between them, it thankfully seemed to have passed.

"Nah," he told her. "Potential fatherhood is at least two million places above those. I mean, alligators have terrible breath, and I read somewhere that hemlock tastes like licorice. I hate licorice."

"Still, you sound like a man who's set on *not* procreating."

"I didn't say that, either," he muttered.

Aha. So she hadn't mistaken the weird ambiguity in him about whether or not he wanted to be a family man.

"Then you *do* want to have kids?" she asked. She wasn't sure why she wanted a clear answer to the question, but for some reason, she did.

That panicked look came over him again, though not quite to the degree it had the first time. Instead of answering, though, he jumped back to the first part of their exchange. "The reason I was here to see Dr. Chavez today is because I was hoping she'd help me out with that project I mentioned that I'm trying to get off the ground."

Fine. They could change the subject. For now. "What kind of project?"

"It's something I'm doing to honor my birth mother, since she—"

"Shelby Fortune!"

She looked up at the sound of her name and saw a different medical assistant holding open the door to the inner examining rooms. She lifted a hand to identify herself, then quickly stood and gathered up her purse, tucking her feet back into her shoes as she did so. Cameron stood, too, then walked with her as far as the door.

"Good luck back there," he told her.

"Thanks," she replied, the flutter of nerves in her belly reflected in her voice, too. "And thanks again for all your help earlier. And for keeping me company."

"It was my pleasure."

Although it was the kind of platitude people normally muttered in reply without thought, the way Cameron said it made it sound as if he truly meant it. That spending a little time with someone he'd just met—someone who had nearly passed out in his arms then spilled a sordid abandoned-after-an-unexpected-pregnancy story all over him—had honestly been enjoyable.

They stood toe to toe for a moment, neither seeming to know what to say. Only when the medical assistant cleared her throat did they both snap out of it. Shelby turned to make her way through the door, but Cameron stopped her with a gentle hand on her arm. When she looked at him again, he was extending a business card he'd withdrawn from somewhere. Automatically, she took it from him.

"Let me know how everything goes," he said, sounding a little nervous himself. "And if you need someone to talk to later, I'm here."

Meaning that if, in the very miniscule likelihood that something not good turned up in the ultrasound, he, a near perfect stranger, would be there to lend an ear.

"Thanks," she said softly. "I will."

He nodded once, then, gripping his Stetson in both hands, he turned and made his way toward the office exit. Shelby kept hoping he would turn around and look at her again, maybe lift a hand in farewell, and throw her one of those mouthwatering smiles. Instead, he just kept going. He pulled open the door, stepped through it and disappeared into the hallway on the other side without a single glance back.

As she followed the assistant back to an examining room, Shelby reminded herself she'd known him for less than an hour, and he really was, for all intents and purposes, a stranger. A near perfect one, to be sure—in more ways than one—but a stranger nonetheless. One who'd made clear he wasn't interested in being a father. Who, in fact, had looked kind of…horrified…by the very suggestion. And she was a woman whose life was about to be consumed by motherhood. Cameron Waite was a nice guy, to be sure. But he was one who was in no hurry to have a family.

And she was still stinging from the last guy she'd welcomed into her life. Dylan hadn't wanted to be a father, either. Something Shelby hadn't discovered until after she'd given him her trust and her loyalty and her heart, only to have all three crushed under his feet. No way was she going to risk that again. Especially when she was going to be responsible not just for her own happiness from now on, but for her child's, too.

"Dr. Chavez will meet you in examining room three," the woman told her.

Shelby nodded fiercely. "I'm ready," she assured her.

As Cameron fled the doctor's office—yes, *fled*, he realized shamefully—he hoped his alarm and urgency hadn't been obvious to Shelby Fortune. Then he remembered she was sharp as a tack. No way could she have *not* noticed. Hell, had he even told her goodbye? He couldn't remember now. It had been all he could do not to turn around and wave one last time, which would have been the polite thing to do, but he'd been afraid the panic that had nearly swamped him with her offhand question about whether or not he wanted to have children would be all too evident again.

As he stumbled back out onto Emerald Ridge Boulevard, the bright sunlight nearly blinded him, making him feel even more disoriented. He couldn't help it. Shelby's question had caught him completely off guard, and memories had come flooding over him so fast, he hadn't been able to stem the flow.

He knew it hadn't even been two months since he and his ex-fiancée split up, but he'd also thought he would be pretty much over her by now, thanks to the awful way things had gone down. And yeah, okay, he was pretty much over Vanessa. But he wasn't sure he'd ever be over the terrible things she had said to him, just weeks before their wedding. He guessed it was still a little too fresh. And Shelby's question, even though it had been playful, had totally blindsided him.

He leaned back against the wall where she had found support just a little while ago and closed his eyes. Damn… Vanessa. He honestly hadn't thought about her for a couple weeks. He'd been so busy trying to get his new foundation off the ground here in Emerald Ridge that his thoughts had been occupied with other things. Now, though, in the wake of what Shelby had said, it all came crashing back.

The two of them had been mere weeks away from their Christmas wedding when Cameron found out the details of his birth. Although he and Drake had found each other months before that, their actual records from the Texas Royale Adoption Agency, which had essentially been sell-ing babies to the highest bidder behind the front of being a legit adoption agency, had been part of a police investigation into it and unavailable to view. Once that investigation concluded, he and his twin brother had finally been given the actual files. They'd learned their birth mother's name and, with some poking around, discovered even more. How Rue Evans had been a poor teenage girl, barely eighteen years old. How she'd been so hurtfully dumped by her baby's father that she didn't even name him on the birth certificate. How she'd been tossed out of her family home by parents that wanted nothing more to do with her.

He supposed he shouldn't have been surprised to learn any of that. It was a story as old as time. But Cameron had been surprised. Even more so than he'd been when he first learned he had a brother out there in the world in the form of Drake Fortune.

He'd always known he was adopted. His parents had never tried to hide that from him and had in fact told him he was even more loved and wanted than most kids because of it, because they'd *chosen* him. But *adoption* had always been some amorphous, vague condition that just kind of felt like a different way of being born. Sure, he'd wondered from time to time about his birth parents, the same way pretty much all adopted kids did. Vaguely, he might have even thought a few times about whether he had other siblings. But none of that had felt real. Jim and Helen Waite *were* his parents. They were his family. Even if sometimes, in some ways, he'd always felt different from them. His adoption had just served to give him an explanation as for why that was, and why what his folks wanted for his future didn't always coincide with what he wanted for himself.

He'd still always felt loved and welcome. And he'd still felt as if the three of them were family. Maybe not by blood, but through love and sharing and togetherness.

And when Cameron finally did get to know Drake and introduced him to Vanessa and his future in-laws, everyone had been delighted by how it all worked out. Drake was a successful oilman just like Vanessa's father was. Like Cameron's adopted family, Drake's also came from wealth and had an impeccable pedigree. They all shared the same kind of background, and they all moved in the same kind of social circles. The trouble came when Cameron found out the actual circumstances of his birth. Rue's meager origins and lack of education. Her unstable homelife and father's alcoholism. Her state of single motherhood and lack of prospects.

None of that had mattered to Cameron or Drake, of course. Knowing their birth mother had overcome so much hardship and made such a huge sacrifice in surrendering her children so they could have a better life than the one she would have given them just made them love her even more. To Cameron, Rue Evans was a hero. To Vanessa and her family, however…

Cameron would never in a million years have suspected the ugliness that lay beneath his fiancée's beautiful, intelligent, sophisticated facade. There had never been a glimmer that she was anything but kind and sweet, smart and funny. Then again, he'd never really seen her out of her regular environment of wealth and privilege.

But with Vanessa and her family, it went even deeper than elitism. Some of the things she'd said to him after she learned about his birth origins had been unforgivable. Yes, she'd known he was adopted, she told him, but she'd never really realized what that meant until she learned the specifics and gave it more thought. Now that she had, she'd realized *his* bloodline wasn't the *true* Waite bloodline, the way it was for his parents.

Those Waites, she'd said, were scions of Dallas society. But Cameron couldn't say that about himself. He wasn't a *real* Waite. His bloodline was… Ahem. His mother was just some poor urchin who had nothing going for her—*I mean, did she even graduate from high school?*—and Cameron's father… Well, Cameron didn't even know who his father was. He could be a criminal. Or a janitor or trash collector or something. Ew.

She couldn't possibly risk tainting her own family tree with that kind of thing. Who knew what kind of damaged DNA was flowing through Cameron's veins? Hers was a founding family of Texas and the pinnacle of Dallas society. She couldn't mingle her pristine line with some vulgar riffraff. Surely, he must understand that.

Cameron understood, all right. Understood that the woman he'd always thought lit up a room every time she entered it actually had a heart and a soul darker than the deepest abyss. But as bad a taste as Vanessa had left in his mouth, he was grateful to her for showing him who she really was before he married her.

In spite of how wrong she was about everything, Cameron would be lying if he said her words hadn't cut him deep. Or that they weren't still bouncing around inside him, as evidenced by his reaction to Shelby's innocent question today. Maybe the reason he'd always felt different from the cream of Dallas society when he was growing up—and hell, even as an adult now—was because he *was* different. Although he'd never been bullied or ostracized or anything else, there had always been a part of him that had never been—and still never was—comfortable in that environment. A part of him that felt like he didn't belong.

Although his parents had brought him up the same way all his friends and fellow students had been raised, and he'd always been welcomed everywhere he went, he'd just never felt like he was a part of that world. Maybe there was something in people's DNA that went beyond stuff like height and eye color and an aptitude for certain things?

If so, maybe on some weird level, Vanessa was right. He really was different from the people he was surrounded by in Dallas. Not worse than them, necessarily. Not better, either. Just different. Ever since realizing that, he'd felt even more at odds with where he really belonged. And until he did figure that out, he just wasn't sure how he was supposed to move forward.

He blew out a restless breath and pushed himself away from the wall. Too many dark thoughts for such a bright, beautiful day. Unbidden, Shelby Fortune's smiling face rose to the forefront of his mind, and he grinned as he began to make his way down the street to where he'd parked. Hers was a much nicer image than Vanessa's to have lingering in his head. But Shelby was part of his ex-fiancée's world, too, when he got right down to it. Like Vanessa's family, the Fortunes were one of the most preeminent in Texas. Maybe *the* most preeminent. Shelby's father was worth billions. She was the product of—and thrived in—a world that he wasn't sure he wanted to be a part of anymore. Even if she wasn't pregnant, it probably wasn't a good idea to think too much about her from here on out. Though a smile like hers was pretty unforgettable.

Cameron forced himself to push all thoughts of Shelby out of his head and fill it instead with all the things he had left to do today. Problem was, he couldn't quite remember what most of those things were now.

Chapter Three

Shelby followed the assistant back to the examining room and changed out of her street clothes and into all the paper regalia laid out for her. She'd just hopped up on the table when there was a soft rap at the door. She gave the all clear, and Dr. Chavez entered, looking her usual stunning self with her close-cropped silver hair and perfect cat eyeliner and gigantic beaded earrings. An official-looking white doctor coat was thrown over a less-official-looking cherry red minidress and brightly colored scarf.

"Hello, Shelby," she said warmly. "How are you feeling?"

They exchanged the usual back-and-forth that went with her regular appointments, including Shelby's explanation that Dylan wouldn't be joining them today, again, but this time it was because he was dust in the wind. As they awaited the arrival of the sonographer, Dr. Chavez went over what she could expect with the procedure. She mentioned that while the image might not look very clear to Shelby, the technology was amazing—capable of detecting so much, even this early in a baby's development.

Then, out of nowhere, the doctor said, "So I saw you

sitting with that nice Cameron Waite out in the waiting room. Are you and he friends?"

"We just met today," Shelby told her. "But he mentioned he's working with you on some kind of project. He didn't get a chance to tell me about it, though."

"Well, it's wonderful," Dr. Chavez said. "And it's not like it's any big secret, so I can tell you something about it. It's a very generous and ambitious program he's putting together called Bedrock. It's a foundation to help impoverished expectant mothers who don't have support from family or friends to help them out. The plan is to give them and their babies a head start in life by covering all their medical expenses and essentials for their homes that they wouldn't be able to afford otherwise. Anything they need, completely free of charge."

Shelby knew she shouldn't be surprised by what the physician told her. Cameron had been nothing but generous and kind to her since meeting her. But even the noblest of men seldom developed projects for women in need. Expectant moms seeking support just didn't tend to be on the radars of most guys. Then she remembered what he'd said about his birth mother. How she came from a poor family that "didn't do right by her." Meaning they probably threw her out when they found out she was having a baby without having a husband first, something that happened all too often. Sure, times were changing about things like that, but change came slowly to a lot of places. And there would always be people who were judgmental and holier-than-thou, no matter where a person went.

In other circumstances, she might very well have ended up in the same place Cameron's mother had, with no one to care for her and her children and no visible means of support. It was just sheer dumb luck that Shelby had been born into a family who would love and support her, no matter what. She wished every woman could be as lucky as she was. *Note to self: write a hefty check for Cameron's new project, as soon as you find out where to send one.*

"His own mother came from rather meager beginnings," Dr. Chavez continued. "It's something he talks about very frankly in the literature for the organization. I have some pamphlets up at the front desk he left for distribution. I'll include one with your other info after the sonogram. It's remarkable what he's taken on. He told me I'm the fifth doctor he's asked to get involved, and so far, every one of them has come on board. I did, too, of course. He's a very persuasive young man," she added with a smile.

That surprised Shelby not at all. Cameron Waite was the very definition of charming. But all she said was, "Wow."

"That man is working fast to get this thing up and running," the doctor continued. "He wants to eventually have dozens of offices and clinics up and running all over the state so that no woman will be more than a short drive or bus ride away from services."

"He really has thought of everything," Shelby said.

"Believe me, he's just getting started," Dr. Chavez told her. "He's determined to honor his birth mother the way he wished he'd been able to do when she was still alive."

Shelby was about to ask more, but there was another soft rap at the door from the sonographer, who pulled a cart in behind herself filled with all kinds of electronic paraphernalia. The sonogram went off without a hitch and without a single sign of anything out of the ordinary. Her son—she was having a boy!—was at exactly the stage of development he should be at this point, Dr. Chavez told her, and, judging by the look of him, he was going to be a handsome lad to boot.

Certainly Shelby couldn't disagree with that last remark. But not because of the image on the screen, which was black-and-white and more than a little fuzzy. But Dylan, for all his many faults, had been very easy on the eyes. And, well, all modesty aside, former Miss Texas and third runner-up for Miss America here.

In spite of the blurriness of the image, tears pricked Shelby's eyes at this first look at her child. Then, little by little, those tears began to flow freely. Now that she looked closer, she thought maybe she did discern a slight resemblance to herself from the image. Maybe she was just imagining it, but still. In profile, her baby seemed to have her nose. And the same sturdy hands she had. And wait, did he have the same beauty mark high on his right cheekbone that she had? Or was it just a spot on the screen?

I'm having a son, she marveled. She suspected her father would be particularly delighted by that, since she'd always sensed he would have liked to have a son in addition to his two daughters. Not that he'd ever made Shelby and Jillian feel like they weren't enough, but… Sometimes he'd said or done other things that gave her the impression that he would have liked to have a larger family, especially one with a boy.

Which, she had always found herself thinking at such times, was kind of odd, considering how little time he spent with the one he had.

"A boy," she said aloud, her voice soft and awestruck

as she looked at her son. She swiped her tears away, but more followed. Any worries she might have still had about motherhood fled, to be replaced by excitement and happiness at what her—and her baby's—future held.

"A boy," Dr. Chavez reaffirmed. "A healthy, hardy baby boy who, judging by the look of his mother, will be very much loved."

Shelby nodded. "He's already very much loved."

Dr. Chavez smiled. "Yes, he is."

She exhaled a slow, shaky breath. Her son was fine. Looking at his blurry image, though, everything suddenly became crystal clear. She was going to have a baby. Her life was going to change in ways she couldn't yet imagine. She had to tell her family now. She had to let her mother and father and sister know that there would be another Fortune living under their roof. Soon.

Then she remembered her father wouldn't be back from his business trip to New York for another two days. She was going to have to sit on the news a while longer, since she really wanted them all to be present for the announcement. Suddenly, she brightened. That gave her time to plan something really cute for the big reveal. Maybe she'd get one of those cakes from Emerald Ridge Bakery that they did for gender reveal parties. White icing on the outside, blue or pink on the inside. She could even try to make up her mind on a name from the three lists she'd started shortly after realizing she was pregnant—one with boy names, one with girl names, and one with gender-neutral names. Shelby had kind of been favoring the gender-neutral ones when she didn't know whether she was having a daughter or son, but now she might take a closer look at the boy names. Or maybe she'd start a new list with all kinds of names on it, because today felt like a whole new start.

"Everything looks great," Dr. Chavez said. "If you want to get dressed and head back out to reception, we'll get your visit summary together and give you a list of what to keep an eye out for between now and your next appointment. You can make one for a month from now. Oh, and I'll be sure to tell reception to include the materials about Cameron's foundation."

"Thanks, Dr. Chavez," Shelby said.

The doctor smiled. "I hope any worries you might have been having are gone now. Your baby truly is right where he needs to be."

Shelby nodded, and whatever lingering fears she'd had began to disappear. Her baby was fine. She was fine. Everything was going to be okay. From here on out, it would be nothing but blue skies ahead.

Cameron's phone began to ring just as he inserted his key into the front door of his penthouse in the heart of downtown. He pulled it out of his pocket long enough to see that it wasn't a number from his contacts, so he let it go to voicemail and tucked it back into his pocket again. Pushing open the door, he stepped through, tossing the correspondence he'd gathered from the lobby mailbox onto the foyer table as he passed it. Although he'd closed on this place a month ago, he still considered home—technically—to be the Waite family mansion in Dallas where he'd grown up. He'd inherited it from his folks after their deaths, and out of a sense of duty, had moved back into the very room he'd occupied as a boy. Though he had at least taken down the posters for Sonic the Hedgehog and Green Day and replaced them with images of Dallas landmarks.

He'd mostly bought this place as a second home once he began to realize how much time he would be spending here. It was a massive penthouse, more room than he needed really, but still not even half the size of the house in Dallas. And where his childhood home was filled with warmth and personal touches from the life he and his parents had lived, this place was filled with…

He looked at it with a critical eye. It was a beautiful place, professionally decorated with neutral colors and boxy, minimalist furnishings. All the accents were Southwestern, from the Navajo rugs to the terra-cotta lamps to the artwork of mesas and wide-open ranges. And it could have belonged to *anyone*. There wasn't one thing here that made it feel like it was his. Nothing that made it feel like home.

It really wasn't easy juggling two places the way he had been. And he still wasn't sure why he'd bought a place in Emerald Ridge when the bulk of his life was back in Dallas. He could have just rented a place here for a while, until he got Bedrock up and running. For that matter, he could run Bedrock as easily from his office at Waite Financial as he could here. He'd just liked the idea of having the heart of the organization in a place where his mother's heart had been, too.

And after realizing Drake was all the family he had left in the world, Cameron had wanted to be closer to him and get to know him like, well, a brother. And maybe make some memories with him that the two of them had been denied as kids. Of course, now Drake was busy with his new wife and baby, but that just cemented Cameron's desire to stay close even more. His twin's family was his family, too, now. He wanted to be the fun uncle to their little one and any other kids the two might have in the future. Between the deaths of Cameron's parents five years ago just before Thanksgiving and his broken engagement just prior to Christmas, he'd been dreading the arrival of holidays from here on out, certain he would have to spend them alone with nothing but bad memories. Now that wasn't the case. With Drake and Annelise and their baby, Cameron had a family again. He didn't want to lose them the way he'd lost everyone else.

As he was sitting down with a beer, his phone chimed again, this time with a text message notification. When he picked it up, he realized it was the same number that had called him a few minutes ago. This time, though, he knew exactly who it was from. This in spite of the fact that it was just three words: It's a boy.

Shelby. Doing exactly what he'd asked her to do. He took a minute to include her in his contacts, then gave her a call back.

"Congratulations," he said when she answered.

"Thanks," she replied. Her voice was as soft and warm as he remembered, threaded now with the kind of happiness that came after a heavy load had been lifted. "He's right where he should be, Dr. Chavez said. He weighs around six ounces, and he's about the size of a baked potato. So, for now, I'm calling him Spud."

Cameron laughed. "You realize you're never going to come back from that, right? He's going to be 'Spud' for the rest of his life. Under his senior picture, it's gonna say 'Class President, NHS, Debate Club. Ambition, Supreme Court Justice. Nickname, Spud.'"

Shelby laughed, too, and something inside him that had still been wound a little too tight after all the day's bad memories slowly eased. "I don't think he'll go into law," she said with much conviction. "I think he's going to be a doctor. And a firefighter on the weekends."

"Ah."

"He'll also be an architect and teach first grade and grow non-GMO food on his organic farm."

"Gotcha."

"And he'll be a movie star and a scientist and possibly a prime minister of some kind. Still working on that part. Because he is most definitely going to be the person who brings about world peace."

"Sounds like Spud's going to be a busy, well-accomplished guy."

"Ya damn right."

There was a moment of silence, where neither seemed to know what to say. So Cameron asked, "Did you go home and tell your family the good news?"

There was a restless sigh from the other end of the line. "I really wanted to wait until my father gets back from his trip to New York day after tomorrow," she said. "But now that I've had the ultrasound, I'm about to burst with the news. I've been sitting here for the last hour just staring at the images, and I want to show them off. And it's not even like I'm a proud mama looking at his first school photos. It could be a hamster in there for all the detail you can see. But Jillian isn't home, and my mother has her book club tonight. It can wait a bit longer."

There was another restless sound.

"Oh, who am I kidding? I think I'm going to go ahead and tell my mother and sister tomorrow morning before they have a chance to take off for the day. We can all meet Daddy at the front door with the news when he gets home. Maybe have some balloons and cupcakes with blue sprinkles or something. He'd get a kick out of that. Yeah," she said with a hint of satisfaction. "I like that idea. I'll tell Mama and Jillian tomorrow morning, first thing."

Cameron smiled. "Sounds like you and your dad are pretty close. He must be a good guy."

There was the merest hesitation from the other end of the line before she replied, "Yeah, he is, I guess."

Her response surprised him. "You guess he's a good guy? You don't know one way or another?"

Now she made a sound of annoyance, though whether it was for herself or her father, he couldn't say.

"To be honest," she said, "sometimes I feel like I don't really know him all that well. He wasn't around a lot when Jillian and I were little because he was always working. And then he and Mama sent us both off to boarding school when we were twelve and eleven. So we never really spent much time with him. He and I have always gotten along fine, but we're not that close. He's just…" Another sigh of exasperation. "Yes, he's a good guy," she finally told him. "Just not one I know all that well."

"I get that," Cameron said. "My dad was pretty busy, too, when I was growing up. He didn't really travel that much, but he worked his ass off all day every day. He still always made it to the important stuff, though. He was there when my high school track team went to state and for opening night of the senior play when I was Willy Loman in *Death of a Salesman*. All three of us did the college tour thing together, and he never missed trick-or-treating with me or a single birthday party."

"That sounds so nice," she said, her voice laced with wistfulness. "See, my dad never did any of those things with me or Jillian. I mean, he made it to a couple of my pageants when I was competing if they happened to coincide with wherever he was, but that's about—"

"Wait, what?" Cameron interrupted, stunned. "Pageants? Like…beauty pageants?"

There was a small sound of surprise from the other end of the line, followed by a soft chuckle. "Oh, wow. We never covered that this morning, did we? I guess I'm so used to people around here knowing how involved I am in the pageant community that I didn't think to mention it."

"You've actually competed in beauty pageants?" he asked, not quite able to mask his surprise.

"Okay, number one, they're not *technically* 'beauty' pageants anymore," she told him, her voice now tinted with what he could only call defensiveness. "There's a lot more to the pageant experience than physical appearance. There's scholarship and leadership and talent and community service. There's always a cause you work toward—mine has always been childhood literacy, because I was such a huge reader when I was a kid first starting out—and a million other things. Pageant participants do a lot more than just walk around in a sparkly tiara. Though, okay, I admit that part is a lot of fun," she added with another laugh. "It's just not the only part."

Properly chastened—but still grinning—Cameron said, "Right. I stand corrected. So what do you do these days? Coach? Judge?"

Now she uttered a sound of disbelief. "Hello? Still competing, thank you very much. Former Miss Texas here, bucko. And third runner-up for Miss America not so long ago."

"Oh, wow. I really do stand corrected."

"Yeah. I've competed since I was ten. I really am kind of a big deal around here."

Cameron told himself he shouldn't be surprised, but he was. Not just that Shelby was beauty pageant —excuse him, *pageant*—material, but that pageants even still existed these days. And she was a former Miss Texas? An almost-Miss-America? Then he remembered how bubbly and personable and charming she was—not to mention drop-dead gorgeous—and it all made perfect sense.

"Or, at least, I *was* kind of a big deal around here," she continued, her voice decidedly less enthusiastic now. "After last week…"

She trailed off before finishing the statement, something Cameron probably should have taken as a clue that she didn't want to continue. But he was finding this side of Shelby Fortune fascinating and didn't want to let it go yet. He'd never met a pageant queen before. She might even know how to twirl a baton. Maybe even a baton that was *on fire*. Was that even a real thing, or did they only do that in movies? He suddenly had to know.

"What happened last week?" he asked before he could stop himself.

She sighed again. "The evening gown segment, that's what happened."

"What? Did you trip over your hem?"

"I wish it had just been that. That I've done, and it can be dealt with fine. No, this… I never saw this coming."

Cameron said nothing, only waited, because he could tell it was something she actually *did* want to talk about.

Just on her terms, not his. After another long exhale, she continued.

"I found this fabulous ruched sheath dress with an absolutely gorgeous scalloped neckline—in peacock blue chiffon no less, which is my signature color—and it fit like a glove."

Cameron didn't know what any of that meant, but he'd bet a million bucks that Shelby had looked like a million bucks wearing it.

"And it was by Ethan Chatto, a Texas designer who's super up-and-coming. I mean, this dress was incredible, and the way Ethan fit it and styled it on me, I looked incredible."

He loved how matter-of-fact she was about her beauty. Like it was simply a truth she'd accepted—that she was stunning—but without thinking it made her in any way better or more important than anyone else. It was just a simple fact of her life, and she was totally comfortable with it. Everyone had a gift, Cameron knew. For some, it was creating art. For others, it was fixing cars. Or remodeling kitchens. Or growing things. But for some—like Shelby—it was being beautiful, outside *and* in.

He smiled as he told her, "I thought you said it wasn't about physical appearance."

"Yeah, well, now I'm the one who stands corrected. There is, of course, some importance placed on how you present yourself physically. And the evening gown competition is my favorite for that. But I guess the judges didn't share my opinion of myself that night. They pointed out every single flaw—what *they* considered flaws, anyway—and they did it while I was right there on the stage in El

Paso, with two dozen other women behind me, and thousands seated in the theater in front of me."

"Flaws?" Cameron echoed. "How could they find flaws with you in your signature peacock blue that fit like a glove?"

"That's what makes me so mad now that I look back on it," she said. "What they considered flaws, I consider my best features ever. Yeah, my body has gotten wider with my pregnancy, but honestly, I think I look better now than I ever did before. Just because curves aren't the traditional beauty standard that's been held over women's heads for the last hundred years… I mean, who came up with these supposed standards anyway? Men, that's who."

Uh-oh. Cameron was suddenly on the wrong side of this conversation, even though he'd had nothing to do with dictating modern beauty standards. Maybe he really shouldn't have pried…

"I mean, I shouldn't care, right?" she continued. "Who wants to be the inaugural Miss Texas Incandescence anyway, if they're gonna stoop as low as calling out women on stage about what *they* perceive to be defects? I swear, Cameron, being a woman in this country nowadays, I might as well just wrap myself in cellophane and throw myself in with the beef shanks and ham hocks at H-E-B."

He laughed out loud at that. Forget twirling a flaming baton. Her contribution to the talent portion must have been stand-up comedy.

"I think you're right," he told her. "You're better off without them. They're the ones who are missing out, not having you as their ambassador."

"Thank you. Anyway, sorry. I didn't mean to hijack the conversation about our fathers and make it all about me.

It's great that you had your dad around for all the things that counted," she said wistfully. "He sounds like he was a good guy himself."

"The best," Cameron agreed.

At least, his adoptive father had been. His birth father on the other hand…

A flash of resentment shot through him when he thought about how his father had abandoned his mother when she was at her most vulnerable. There was a special place in hell for people who turned their backs on the ones who loved and needed them most.

"I should probably let you get back to whatever you were doing," she said. "I didn't mean to bend your ear all night."

"I'm glad you called," he told her. "And I'm glad everything went well with the sonogram. Sounds like Spud is in good hands."

"It will be good to tell Mama and Jillian tomorrow," she said. "And start making plans to announce it to Daddy. Maybe having a grandbaby will slow him down some and keep him closer to home for a change."

"Maybe so."

"It'd be nice to finally spend some time with him."

Cameron thought about his own dad again. He really had been great about trying to be as involved as he could with his son's upbringing, and Cameron was grateful for that. But there had always been a part of him that wondered if maybe his father's involvement had been more about molding his son into the man he expected him to become than celebrating Cameron's own wants and needs for developing into the person *he* wanted to be. There had been more than one conversation about how important it was to be realistic about the future and focus on things that would contribute to a stable, fiscally responsible tomorrow and how Waite Financial was just waiting for him to take over someday.

Of course you were great in the play, Cam, but let's not go overboard with this drama thing when you really need to spend more time with Future Business Leaders of America.

Running around is fine for physical fitness, son, but those hours you spend with the track team could be better spent with the Finance Club.

Why on earth would you want to start a gay-straight alliance at school, Cam, when your school doesn't even have a DECA chapter yet? Spearheading that instead would be much more impressive on your college applications.

He knew his dad had always wanted what was best for him. But sometimes Cameron had wondered if his father had wanted what was best for himself and Waite Financial more.

"I hope you and your dad have nothing but good times ahead," he told Shelby now.

"Me, too," she replied softly.

"Congratulations again on little Spud," Cameron told her. "I'm already looking forward to attending his first birthday party."

"Be there or be square."

There was another moment of silence where neither seemed to know what to say. Or maybe it was just that neither wanted to say goodbye. Which was weird. Cameron wasn't usually someone who liked to talk on the phone. He much preferred texting and email. When he did have to make calls, he kept them short and to the point, then hung up as soon as he could. With Shelby, though…

It was just nice talking to her, that was all. He couldn't remember the last time he'd actually enjoyed a conversation as much as the two he'd had with her.

"You take it easy, Shelby," he finally told her.

"You, too, Cameron."

"Guess I'll see you around town."

"Guess so."

More silence. More not saying goodbye.

"Maybe we can have coffee sometime," he told her.

"I'd like that," she replied.

"Well, all right, then. It's a…"

Don't say date, he told himself. *Do not say* date.

"An ambiguous plan for the future," she finished with a laugh when the moment began to stretch out.

"My favorite kind," he assured her.

"Mine, too."

"Good night, Shelby."

"Good night, Cameron."

Even finally getting out the words to end the conversation, Cameron didn't want to be the one to hang up. He waited to see if Shelby would do it first, but she didn't disconnect the call, either. This was ridiculous. It wasn't like they'd never see each other or speak again. He placed his thumb over the button to hang up just as he heard the line click closed on her end. And as much as he wanted to, somehow, he managed to not tap her number to dial her again.

Chapter Four

The house where Shelby and her sister, Jillian, grew up and continued to live had always been filled with warmth and laughter and love. The two-level Mediterranean Revival style sprawled over nearly five thousand square feet on each floor and had been built in the 1920s by the first cattle rancher to settle in the area, long before Emerald Ridge became the bustling community it was now. Her parents had bought it before the sisters were born, because Archibald had passed it often when he was a child, gazing upon it with awe, amazed that anyone could actually live in such a huge, majestic place. For the little boy who grew up on a tiny crumbling ranch on the wrong side of the tracks, it might as well have been a magic castle filled with dragon treasure. Her father snatched it up the minute the previous owners put it up for sale, without even asking the price, then hired a professional to furnish the place with period pieces and accents. Living in their house, her father had always said, had felt like living in a dream come true.

It was kind of a dream for Shelby, too. She was glad to be home after living for nine months with Dylan in his condo—which, in spite of her best efforts to put her own personal stamp on it, had never really felt like home. She loved this house as much as her father did and couldn't wait to start making memories here with her son. Holidays, especially, had always been enchanting, with the Thanksgiving table piled high with every traditional food her mother read about in magazines—and which were prepared by their cook, Mrs. Pulaski—and Christmas trees were nestled into a corner of every room they used. The expansive front and back yards outside had hosted Easter egg hunts in the spring and pool parties in the summer, always with the green hills of Emerald Ridge and her father's cavorting horses as a backdrop.

Of course, for most of those holidays and events, Archibald had been nowhere around, because holidays and summers were the busiest time for the airline industry. He'd had to be where all the hot spots were during those times, but he'd always promised to make it up to the girls when he got home. And he did his best, lavishing on them extravagant gifts from his travels and treating them to belated celebrations with an expensive dinner in town. Still, it would have been nice to have him around more often. The Fortune family home would have felt even homier with Archibald actually in it.

This morning, as Shelby descended the stairs, still in her pajamas, that familiar sense of *Daddy-isn't-home* settled over her again. Though today, for some reason, it felt even heavier than usual. When she entered the kitchen with its soaring white cabinetry and gold accents, she found her mother sitting at the spacious maple-topped island, staring at the phone she'd placed in front of herself as if waiting for it to magically turn into a bouquet of roses. She was still in her pajamas, too, her silver-threaded dark hair piled loosely atop her head, a cup of coffee sitting neglected beside the phone. She hadn't even noticed her daughter coming in.

"Mama? Is everything okay?" Shelby asked.

Her mother glanced up at the question, looking startled to realize she wasn't alone. "I just had a strange call from Hamish Inland."

Shelby recognized the name. "Daddy's attorney?"

Her mother nodded, the gesture looking oddly mechanical. "Hamish is in Emerald Ridge and needs to speak to us this morning."

"Us?" Shelby echoed.

"Yes, you and Jillian, too. He wanted to make sure all three of us were home before he came over."

"What's he doing in Emerald Ridge?" she asked. "Doesn't Daddy usually see him in Dallas or Houston or someplace?"

"In Dallas, usually. But Hamish has been to the house a time or two before."

Shelby remembered one such occasion herself, when she was a teenager. She came home from a shopping trip in town one summer and passed her father's home office on the way to her bedroom to find him and his attorney engaged in conversation about something. What Shelby remembered most was how it had been super-hot that day, but Mr. Inland had been buttoned up in a flawless pinstriped suit with nary a hair out of place. This in spite of the fact that her father had been dressed in Bermuda shorts and a Guayabera shirt.

"But Mr. Inland has only been here when Daddy was home," Shelby said. "Why does he want to see all three of us?"

"I have no idea. He didn't say. Only that he'd be over

in about an hour." She finally seemed to see Shelby for the first time. "We need to get dressed, dear."

"What about Jillian?" Her sister was usually up with the sun.

"I caught her on her way out," her mother said. "She has an errand to run in town, but she assured me she'd be back by ten, when Hamish said he would be here."

"Okay," Shelby said. "That at least gives me time to eat something."

The last thing she needed was a repeat of yesterday's lightheadedness. Even if that had led to a pretty nice outcome in meeting Cameron Waite.

Even thoughts of Cameron, though, couldn't chase away the odd feeling of disquiet that settled over the entire house as the arrival of Hamish Inland loomed. Shelby's thoughts were a tumble of unease as she munched on a slice of tasteless toast and sipped her herbal tea, growing more agitated as she dressed in a sage-colored peasant dress and wove her hair into a loose braid. When she went back downstairs, she just couldn't shake a feeling of impending doom.

And judging by her mother's and sister's demeanors when she joined them in the living room, they were just as uneasy as she was. Whatever the attorney had to tell them, it couldn't be good. Otherwise, her father would have been coming here with him.

For some reason, she couldn't quite quell the thought of some kind of financial disaster. Like maybe Fortune Air had somehow gone bankrupt and Archibald was afraid to tell the family himself, so he sent Mr. Inland to do it. Or, worse, he'd not only fallen into financial straits, but taken off for parts unknown, leaving them all to face the consequences without him. She chastened herself for thinking that last part. Maybe she didn't know her father all that well, but she knew enough about him to realize he would never abandon them. Especially in the worst of circumstances. If there was bad news to be had, he would be the one to deliver it, and he would face the repercussions himself.

So what could be major enough that Hamish Inland needed to say it to her father's family in person, without Archibald present? What on earth was going on?

As if summoned by the thought, the doorbell rang, the normally cheerful chime sounding kind of ominous in the too-quiet house. Roxie, the Fortunes' live-in housekeeper, was off today, as was Mrs. Pulaski, their cook who came a few nights a week and did meal prep on weekends. Shelby had never really noticed how deep a silence could be until now. Just went to show how much anxiety could infect places as well as people.

Each of the Fortune women looked at each other, but none jumped up to answer. Finally, Shelby said, "I'll get it," and rose to do just that.

Her feeling of impending doom increased when she saw that there wasn't one, but two, visitors on the porch. The first, Mr. Inland, was as dapper as always in a chocolate-colored bespoke suit with a gold shirt and a necktie spattered with what looked like tiny bronze coins. His salt-and-pepper hair was cut short, and tortoiseshell glasses enhanced the blue eyes behind them. The fact that her dad's lawyer looked exactly the same way Shelby remembered the last time she met him would have heartened her had it not been for his companion. Because Mr. Inland was accompanied by Chief Russell Campbell, of the Emerald Ridge PD. Why would

Chief Campbell be here? That didn't make sense. Unless he was there to arrest her father for something? Or to tell them Archibald Fortune was already behind bars?

Oh, Daddy, what have you done?

"Miss Fortune," Mr. Inland greeted her.

She waited for him to say something more, or to at least smile, anything to make her feel less ill at ease. But he did none of those things, which only jacked up her anxiety a few more notches.

"Mr. Inland," she replied. She turned to the other man, but all she could manage by way of a greeting for him was, "Chief Campbell."

He lifted a finger to his wide-brimmed, Smokey-the-Bear hat and simply said, "Miss Shelby." And he looked unusually stern against the otherwise lovely blue of the late morning sky behind him.

After a moment's hesitation, she opened the front door wider and took a few steps back. "Won't you both come in?"

Each man nodded to her as they entered, then preceded her into the living room when she told them that was where her mother and Jillian were waiting. Both women stood as they entered, all exchanging the same kind of clipped greetings with them that Shelby had. Chief Campbell took off his hat, and for some reason, the gesture made Shelby feel even more apprehensive.

"Hamish?" her mother said softly. "What's going on? Why is Russell with you? Where's Archibald?"

"Has Dad done something wrong?" Jillian blurted.

She looked as alarmed as Shelby felt. It was no secret in Emerald Ridge that Jillian and their father hadn't ever really gotten along, and Shelby knew her sister probably considered him an even bigger stranger than she did herself. She still wasn't sure why there had always been so much friction between the two, but she suspected some of it at least was due to the fact the two of them were a lot alike. Brash, outgoing, complete type A's, both of them. Jillian even looked like their father, with her long chestnut waves and hazel eyes framed by the same thick lashes he had.

Instead of answering her, Mr. Inland and Chief Campbell exchanged a brief look. Then the attorney turned to the Fortune women again.

"Agatha, Shelby, Jillian," he said softly, "if I could just have the three of you take a seat."

Shelby wanted to tell him no, to quit stalling and just say whatever he had to say. But her mother and Jillian both retreated to the mauve velvet sofa near the fireplace, so she took her seat in the matching chair beside it. Chief Campbell positioned himself beside the fireplace, arms behind his back in a kind of military at-ease stance. Meanwhile, Mr. Inland moved to a side table, setting his briefcase atop it before unfastening the clasps on it, the soft *clicks* sounding like pops from a child's toy gun in the silent room. It was all Shelby could do not to flinch.

"I'm afraid I have some upsetting news," Hamish said as he withdrew a file folder from inside the briefcase.

He focused his attention on that as he opened it and sifted through some papers, and Shelby couldn't help thinking it was more because he didn't want to look at the Fortune women than it was because whatever was in those papers was important. When he finally did look up, it was to peer over his glasses at each of them in turn, then back down at the papers again.

"It's about Archibald," he said, his voice dropping even lower. "I'm afraid there's been…an incident."

Oh, jeez, Shelby thought. Her father *had* been arrested for something. Whatever it was had to be a mistake. They'd get things sorted out somehow.

"What kind of incident?" their mother asked. "Archibald is in New York. He's due to return tomorrow."

Mr. Inland looked up again. "I'm afraid that won't be happening, Agatha. Archibald has had a heart attack, and—"

"He's in the hospital?" Shelby asked. The relief that poured through her was enormous. No, being in the hospital wasn't good, but it was a darn sight better than being incarcerated.

"Why didn't you just tell me that over the phone?" Agatha said, standing. "Which hospital is he in? I'll book a flight right away. The girls can come with me."

Shelby and Jillian both nodded and started to stand, too, but Mr. Inland raised a hand, urging them all to sit again. With clear reluctance, they all did.

"No," he told them, his tone somber. "I'm afraid the heart attack was fatal. Archibald is gone. He died in his sleep and was found early this morning. One of his attorneys in New York is working with officials there now to have him returned to Emerald Ridge as soon as possible."

Shelby heard all the words the attorney said clearly enough, but they didn't seem able to settle in her brain, instead bouncing around too much for her to grasp any of them. Then, once she finally did, tears sprang to her eyes. Daddy was dead? That was impossible. He was too full of life. He was *larger* than life. Everyone said so. Everyone.

"I'm sorry," Mr. Inland said to the silent room. "It's a

lot to have to absorb so suddenly. And it's a terrible loss to grasp."

Shelby glanced first at the attorney, who appeared to be almost as stunned as the rest of them, then at her mother and sister. They, too, still seemed to be processing the announcement, both looking completely lost, just like Shelby.

And then, as one, all three of them began to object.

"No," Agatha said, her voice soft and shaky. "No, no, no. Archibald can't be gone. He *can't*."

"He was fine when he left last week," Jillian insisted.

"Daddy is the strongest man I know," Shelby added. "This is impossible."

The three of them continued to speak, one over another, none of them seeming to hear a word the others said. About how Archibald had no history of heart problems. About how he took such good care of himself. About how he was only seventy and still working and living like a thirty-year-old.

About how he couldn't possibly be gone.

When Agatha began to cry openly, Shelby moved to the sofa to sit on her other side. In spite of their own shock, she and Jillian both wrapped their arms around their mother, pulling the three of them close together. Mr. Inland withdrew a handkerchief from his jacket pocket and strode to the sofa to hand it to Agatha, who accepted it gratefully, pressing it to her eyes. Then she wept some more.

"I'm so sorry, Agatha," Mr. Inland said again. He looked at the sisters. "Shelby, Jillian, I know how devastating it can be to lose a loved one." To all the women, he continued, "I can scarcely believe the news myself. I've known Archibald for decades. He seemed invincible, as if he would go on long after the rest of us were gone."

Yes, that was exactly how her father had seemed. Shelby couldn't imagine a world without him in it.

Before she and her sister and mother could fall too deeply into their grief, though, Mr. Inland returned to the side table and retrieved the paper he'd been holding before to scan it again. "Ladies, I'm afraid there's more news I have to break to you about Archibald, and it's not particularly good."

Shelby couldn't imagine anything more crushing than hearing that her father had been wrenched from their lives, but the look on the attorney's face made all her apprehension return. She hadn't even begun to process her grief. How could there be more?

"Archibald left behind a letter that he wanted me to read to you all in the event of his death."

Her mother hiccupped with another sob, then dropped the hand holding the hanky into her lap. "Honestly, Hamish, can that not wait a bit? The girls and I need time to—"

"I'm afraid not," Mr. Inland said delicately. "Archibald was quite clear in his instructions, and he wanted this information to be delivered immediately after informing you of his demise."

Agatha looked as if she wanted to object again, but didn't seem to have the wherewithal to do it. She only dabbed at her eyes again and inhaled a deep breath. Tears, however, continued to stream down her cheeks.

Mr. Inland adjusted his glasses, and began to read from the letter, his voice quiet, but resolute. "Before I read what he wanted to tell you, I should also inform you that the three of you are not the only ones privy to the information contained within this letter. My brothers, Carlton and Hans, are with two other families as we speak, one in Dallas and one in Houston, respectively."

Why would her father want the same letter read to two other families besides his own? Shelby wondered. Unless maybe they were the families of trusted colleagues. She supposed that would make sense.

Without clarifying further, the lawyer held up the letter and read aloud. "'To my loved ones upon my death,'" he began. "'Above all else, I am deeply sorry for the heartache this will cause all of you. I have three separate families. Three wives, Agatha, Damaris and Taffy, with whom I have five children—Shelby and Jillian, Hayes and Penn, and Madeline. I have kept you all a secret from one another.'"

"Whoa, whoa, whoa," Jillian said before Shelby could utter words to the same effect. "What does that mean, he has *three* families?"

Instead of replying to her question, Mr. Inland said, "If you'll let me continue, it will all come clear."

Come clear? Shelby echoed to herself. That her father had wives and children in addition to herself, her sister and her mother? She could barely even entertain the possibility of that. She opened her mouth to join in Jillian's protest, but Mr. Inland began to read again.

"'I am leaving my vast fortune to be split equally among my three families, with one caveat. Thirty years ago, despite having three wives and young children, I had an affair in Emerald Ridge with a woman—'"

"An *affair*?" Shelby interrupted. "That's impossible. Our father would never have an affair with another woman." *No,* a little voice at the back of her head piped up, *evidently, he would only* marry *other women.*

"'—who knew I was married,'" Mr. Inland continued, unfazed, "'but not that I had three wives. My mistress told me she was pregnant and wanted me to divorce and marry her.'"

Pregnant, Shelby repeated to herself alone this time. There was another half sibling out there?

Mr. Inland continued to read. Although Shelby's head was starting to spin—in a way that had nothing to do with her own pregnancy—she forced herself to listen to every word. "'Suddenly my long list of lies, deceit and betrayals all became too much for me to bear. I didn't love my mistress the way I love my wives. So, I distanced myself, struggling with what to do. Furious, she ended up uncovering my secret about my bigamy and threatened to expose me unless I paid her millions, which I did. She then disappeared, and I never heard from her again.

"'For my children to inherit my fortune, I require that all five of you work together to find your missing sibling. Upon confirmation of DNA testing, this heir will then inherit a particular parcel of very valuable land in Emerald Ridge that holds the key to my past and may help you all find peace with who your father was. I know this will be hard to believe, but I love you all very much.'" Now Mr. Inland looked up at them again. Softly, he concluded, "The letter is signed 'Archibald Fortune.'"

If someone had just struck Shelby from behind with a two-by-four, she didn't think she would feel any less dazed than she did as the attorney finished reading her father's letter. She hadn't even come to terms yet with the news that Archibald was dead. Now she was learning he had two other families in addition to her own? That she had half siblings out there in the world that she'd never known about? How could any of this be possible?

Then she remembered how often her father had been gone when she and Jillian were children. She recalled all the empty chairs at the table over the years. All the kisses goodbye. They'd all assumed Archibald was gone because he was working. Instead, he'd left them alone so that he could be with another family.

Strangely, the news of her father's bigamy—no, *trigamy*—brought Shelby's grief to a halt. So many other emotions joined it now—confusion, disappointment, betrayal, anger—that all she could feel then was stunned. It was going to take time for all of this to even settle in her brain, never mind her being able to sort through it. Right now, she only felt numb.

She looked at Jillian, who seemed to be as baffled and hurt as she was. Then she looked at her mother. Wow. Mama looked as if she was about to check out of reality entirely. Before Shelby could say a word, however, her mother began to cry in earnest again. Then the sobs turned into howling, which quickly morphed into Agatha swearing—calling Archibald names no genteel Southern woman should even know, let alone speak. And loudly, at that. Really, *really* loudly. Then again, if Shelby had just discovered her husband had done the things her mother had discovered about hers, she doubtless would have had a few choice words, too.

To his credit, Mr. Inland didn't bat an eye. He only let Agatha rant for a moment, until her angry words devolved back into uncontrolled sobbing. Once she did, the attorney cleared his throat.

"There is a final bit of news," he said.

"Oh, no," Shelby said. "*No, no, no, no, no.* I think you've told us more than enough, Mr. Inland. Anything else can wait."

Jillian nodded vehemently. "At least give us the rest of the day to sort through everything you've told us this morning. We can meet again tomorrow—"

"Actually, we *will* be meeting again tomorrow," Mr. Inland interjected. Before any of them could say a word, he continued, "Your father's three families will all be converging here in Emerald Ridge tomorrow to discuss the details of his estate and his last wishes."

"*What?*" the sisters exclaimed in unison.

"Are you serious?" Jillian added.

"That's just going to make things even worse," Shelby said. "For all of us."

"It's what your father wanted," Mr. Inland told them. "And it is my duty to ensure that his instructions are followed. The other two wives and their children will be coming in today from Houston and Dallas, and they'll be staying at the Emerald Ridge Hotel. I've arranged for a conference room there in the morning where all the families and their attorneys can be present to discuss your father's will and any information about a possible sixth heir. I'll email you all with the details."

There was another moment of dumbfounded silence as the Fortune women came to terms with that. Then, with a final dab of her nose with the handkerchief, Agatha sat up straight. "Those women are *not* Archibald's wives," she said with surprising calmness. And with more than a little imperiousness, Shelby couldn't help noting. "*I* am Archibald's wife. Those women are travesties."

Wow. Shelby had never seen her mother stand up for herself like that. *Way to go, Mama.*

To his credit, Mr. Inland dipped his head toward her just the slightest bit, as if to acknowledge what she'd said without actually acknowledging what she'd said. Then he withdrew three file folders from inside his briefcase and fanned them across the end table.

"I've made up a dossier for each of you to give you more information about the other families. Everything within these folders is common knowledge and essential information about each person who will be present tomorrow along with me and my brothers. The other families, in turn, are each receiving a similar dossier about you, along with the other family involved. I would advise you to read over these beforehand so that you may become more acquainted with Archibald's other families and to keep the meeting focused on the terms of his will."

All three women erupted with questions after that, and Mr. Inland evaded every one of them with the kind of tact and facility that could only come with decades of being an attorney for the very rich and powerful. He only reiterated that he would send them the details of tomorrow's meeting and collected his things. Then, as the women followed him, still all talking at once, he and Chief Campbell—who hadn't said a single word the entire time and must have only been present because it was standard operating procedure to have some kind of law enforcement involved in announcing the death of a loved one—made their way to the front door. The women continued to speak as the men made their way through it and down the front steps to where Chief Campbell had parked an

Emerald Ridge PD SUV and climbed into it. Then they kept babbling incessantly even as the vehicle drove away.

Finally, they all must have realized how ridiculous they were being and stopped to simply look at each other in confusion. The silence that fell then was profound, broken only by the incongruous laughing chatter of a canyon wren in a distant cabinet oak tree.

"I can't believe he's gone," Agatha said softly. "What am I going to do without him?"

Shelby and Jillian exchanged a look, both seeming to have the same answer to that question. But where Shelby kept it to herself, her sister, ever the outspoken one, put it right out into the world for everyone to hear.

"The same thing we've always done," she said. "Go about our lives. He was never home anyway."

"Jillian, that's cruel," their mother whispered.

"It's a fact, Mama. Dad was always traveling. And now we know the real reason why. My God, he had two other families besides ours."

"Jillian, please," Agatha said.

Jillian started to say something else—and by her expression, it was going to be another dose of painful truth—so Shelby placed a warning hand on her arm to stop her. Jillian threw her an exasperated look, then gentled some. "I'm sorry Dad is gone," she said more softly. "But he was never really here to begin with."

Shelby wished she could disagree with her sister, but Jillian was right. Although she'd always gotten along with their father better than her sister had, Archibald Fortune truly had been away from the home he loved so much far more than he had been in it. The realization of that only compounded her reaction to his death. Certainly, Shelby would miss him. Of course she would grieve his death. But where a lot of people would feel a huge gaping hole in their lives after losing their father, for the Fortune daughters... Well, it was complicated.

"I'm taking King out for a ride," Jillian said. "I need to clear my head."

Her announcement surprised no one. Jillian and her black Friesian horse, King, went together like James Bond and his Aston Martin. Taking King out for a ride was the way she always dealt with difficult times. Shelby wished she had something similar she could fall back on. She'd always dealt with difficult times by looking for a silver lining of some kind—and almost always finding one. But there was none to be had with something like this.

Their mother began to weep again, lifting Mr. Inland's handkerchief to her nose once more. "I think I'd like to be alone, too," she said.

All three women started to turn back toward the front door, but another vehicle appeared where Chief Campbell's had disappeared only a moment ago, approaching the house this time instead of leaving. A delivery van by the look of it. When it came to a halt where the chief's SUV had been parked, Shelby saw that the logo and lettering on the side identified it as coming from Lone Star Little Ones, an upscale children's boutique in downtown Emerald Ridge. She recognized it because she'd done more than a little browsing in the shop over the last few months. And, okay, maybe she'd made a few discreet purchases, too, telling owner Flora Rodriguez that they were "for a friend."

Hey, she hadn't been lying. She and her baby were going to be the best of friends.

"What the…?" Jillian said from beside her.

The driver, a young woman dressed in khaki coveralls, leaped out of the driver's seat and opened the back of the van, withdrawing a huge gift basket from inside. Seriously, that thing was nearly as big as she was. She took a minute to adjust it so that it wouldn't block her view as she carried it, then carefully made her way up the stairs.

"Hi," she said with a bright smile, obviously having no idea what kind of turmoil currently surrounded the group at the front door. "Is one of you possibly Shelby Fortune?"

"I'm Shelby," she said.

The driver extended the basket toward her. "This is for you, then."

Shelby accepted it automatically, having to do a bit of a dance herself to handle it without dropping it.

"Congratulations!" the driver said brightly. Then she turned and made her way back to the van.

Jillian and her mother looked at Shelby, her mother's tears easing in her obvious confusion. "Congratulations?" she echoed.

Jillian added, "Is there something you want to tell us, Shelby?"

No way was she going to drop the bombshell about her baby to her mother and sister this morning. They'd all been through enough emotional upheaval for one day. Even if the news could possibly bring joy to an otherwise terrible situation, right now just wasn't a good time. There were still too many emotions warring in her head she was sure mirrored her mother's and sister's. She simply could not, would not, add more to the mix. In fact, right now, all she wanted to do was escape to someplace where she could be alone with her thoughts, too, and try to sort through everything she was feeling and what she was going to do next.

"It's not for me," she said evasively. And not lying, because lying would be wrong. Whatever was in this basket was obviously for her baby. What wasn't obvious to her, though, was who it was from, since the only people who knew she was expecting were Dylan—who'd probably forgotten by now that he was even going to be a father, that rat—Dr. Chavez, yesterday's sonographer, and…

And *Cameron Waite.* Who was exactly the kind of person who would send a gift to an anxious woman. Even one he barely knew.

"It's a gift for a friend," she told her still clearly dubious sister. And mother. Because Agatha was giving her an odd look, too. She told herself she still wasn't lying. She and Spud really were going to be joined at the hip while he was growing up, she was certain. "I'll just take this inside, and then I think I'll go out for a little while myself."

She turned away before her family could challenge her reassurances and hurried back into the house. Then she paused just long enough to set the gift basket on the chair in the living room she'd vacated only moments ago—though it almost didn't fit, so large was it. Wrapped in pale blue cellophane, it was filled with enough loot to obscure the entire back of the chair. She peered into the basket long enough to discern that the items inside actually weren't just for her baby. There were also some things in there that would be much appreciated by an expectant mother—a silk sleep mask and neck pillow, a bath bomb and drawer sachet, a box of herbal tea and what looked like a comfy throw. She saw an envelope attached that had her name on it, so quickly untied it and stuffed it into her pocket. There, see? All proof gone that the gift was intended for her. Her sister and mother would never suspect now.

Except that they both looked more than a little suspicious when they came into the room behind her. Shelby tossed each of them a thin smile, then grabbed one of the dossiers Mr. Inland had left on the table and headed past them without another word. She snagged her big hobo bag and a rose-colored cardigan from the peg where she'd hung it in the kitchen, stuffed the dossier inside it, then sprinted for the back door. She was closing it behind herself when she heard her mother call out her name. Quickly, and with a heavy heart, she pretended she didn't hear and shut the door behind herself.

In all honesty, she had no idea where she was going to go. She only knew she needed to be somewhere else. Someplace that wasn't teeming with memories of her father, and that wouldn't remind her of the turbulence facing her tomorrow— meeting her father's other families. Somewhere she could pretend nothing was wrong, and where she could feel reassured that everything would somehow be all right.

Because right now, that was what Shelby needed most of all—a refuge to keep the rest of the world at bay. She hopped into her car and drove to the end of the driveway that connected to the main road…then threw the car into Park, because she had no idea which way to turn.

Something poked her thigh, and she remembered the envelope from the gift basket that she'd tucked into her pocket. Withdrawing it, she pulled the card from inside and read it. *One thing I've learned talking to expectant mothers over the last couple of months is that they deserve as much attention as the little ones they're waiting for. You take it easy, Shelby. All the best, Cameron Waite.*

She smiled as she read over the message a second time. And suddenly, she knew exactly where to turn.

Chapter Five

Cameron had no idea what compelled him to go home for lunch, but when he saw Shelby Fortune sitting on the floor beside his front door, he was more than a little happy that he did. Until he realized she didn't look particularly happy herself. In fact, she didn't even seem to notice his approach. She was leaning against the wall, knees drawn up, arms folded over them, her head resting back with her eyes closed. Another one of those long, flowy dresses, this one the color of the cactus plants his mother grew on their patio, was covering her legs to the floor, and a dark pink sweater covered the top of her. Beside her was an oversize canvas bag of bright yellow, and beneath it was what looked like a file folder with loose pages spilling out.

He drew nearer, waiting for her to react, but she didn't move at all. Even when he stood right next to her, she remained absolutely still. Only when she inhaled deeply and murmured a soft little sound did he realize she was actually asleep. Cameron grinned. He'd spoken to enough pregnant women since undertaking his Bedrock project to know that fatigue was a major byproduct of pregnancy. Not that he was surprised. He was still frankly amazed by the whole concept of one human being able to grow another human being inside themselves—and in only nine months. That they still went about their daily lives while doing it was nothing short of staggering.

He squatted down until his head was almost level with hers. "Shelby," he said softly.

She murmured again, but still didn't wake up.

"Shelby," he repeated, a little louder this time.

When she still didn't stir, he settled a hand lightly on her shoulder. He tried not to notice how warm her skin was beneath the fabric under his palm—truly, he did—but he couldn't help noticing that her skin was really warm beneath the fabric under his palm.

At the gentle touch, she finally turned her head toward his and opened her eyes. She seemed disoriented for a second and gazed at Cameron in confusion. Then, finally, she recognized him.

"Cameron," she said quietly.

"Hey there," he greeted her just as softly. "You okay?"

Her eyes opened wider, and she suddenly seemed to remember exactly where she was. When she scrambled to standing, grabbing her bag and the folder beneath it, Cameron stood, too, taking a step away to give her some room. She stuffed the folder into her bag, slung it over her shoulder, then ran both hands across her face and through the loose hair framing her cheeks in an effort to rouse herself. Their gazes connected for a fleeting moment before she glanced away, her cheeks turning pink.

"I am so sorry. I guess I fell asleep waiting for you."

"How long have you been here?" he asked.

"I don't know. What time is it?"

"Going on noon."

"Gosh, almost an hour, then." She released a breath,

admitting, "I stopped by hoping you'd be home, but there was no answer."

"You should have called me. Or texted."

"I thought about it, but I didn't want to interrupt if you were in an important meeting with someone."

He wanted to tell her she could interrupt him anytime she wanted to but stopped himself. Truth was, an hour ago, he had been in kind of an important meeting with a local contractor who was giving him hell about a children's free clinic Cameron was trying to get built. The costs the guy was quoting were ridiculous, especially for a nonprofit, and he hadn't been the kind of man who would have welcomed an interruption. Especially from an *unwed mother*, the likes of whom the dude clearly did not have any sympathy for, something else he made clear during their conversation. Needless to say, Cameron had ended the meeting right there with a few choice words of his own, but… Yeah. It wouldn't have been the best time for Shelby to have called.

"Anyway," she said, "I thought maybe if I just waited for a bit, you might come home. I didn't mean for it to turn into an hour. And I still don't mean to interrupt your day," she hurried on. "If you're busy, I won't keep you. I just…"

Even though her voice trailed off, Cameron could tell by the look on her face that there was a lot she wanted to say.

"I'm not busy at all," he lied. He'd been planning to catch up with some overdue email while he was home, but hell, it could wait a day longer. "I'm glad you're here. I could use some company. Have you had lunch?"

She shook her head. "I barely had breakfast."

He threw her a teasingly chastising look. "Don't you remember what happened the last time you did that?"

She smiled, but the gesture wasn't quite happy. "Yeah. I fell into the arms of a handsome stranger." Immediately, she blushed. "Oh, my gosh. I cannot believe I said that out loud. Pregnancy hormones," she added. "They're crazy sometimes."

Cameron chuckled. "I'll pretend I didn't hear a thing." Another lie. It had been a while since he'd received a compliment—especially one from a pretty woman. He was going to carry this one around with him for a while.

"Thanks." She smiled again, but it still seemed forced.

"Shelby, is everything okay?"

She shook her head and looked to be on the verge of tears. "No. That's why I came over here. I needed to talk to someone, and for some reason, you popped into my head. You were just so nice yesterday, and so easy to talk to…"

Again, her voice trailed off. Again, he knew that wasn't the end of it. And not just because of what she'd told him, but because of how she looked. Shelby Fortune was beyond tired, he could see. She was exhausted. As if she'd been bearing much too heavy of a load for too long. Not just with her pregnancy, but with a host of other things, too.

"Then you better come inside and sit down," he said as he inserted his key into the front door. "I'll fix you a sandwich. You like BLTs?"

This time when she smiled, it looked a lot more genuine. "I love BLTs," she replied.

He pushed the front door open, then gestured for her to precede him. As he followed her inside, he was struck again by just how bland his place was. Shelby and her outfit were a bright splash of color amid the earth tones, like an early breath of springtime. And hell, winter in Texas wasn't even winter, really. Even so, something about having her in his condo made it feel as if the temperature went up ten degrees and the sunlight streaming through the windows turned golden.

He noticed her looking around as she entered, which was probably what most people did when they went into someone's house for the first time. She seemed to be taking in a lot more details than most people, though, as if she were looking for something in particular and not finding it. Finally, she spun around and met his gaze.

"I remember you saying yesterday you've been dividing your time between Dallas and here. That must be stressful."

He lifted one shoulder and let it drop. "Yeah. But to be honest, I've been spending an awful lot more time in Emerald Ridge than I have in Dallas since Drake and I reconnected. I don't think I'll ever move here permanently, but…"

He hesitated. Mostly because he wasn't sure where he'd been going with whatever he'd intended to say. Even though he had good people in place to run the family business—most of them there since his father's time as CEO—Cameron had still been away from Waite Financial for too long. Certainly Bedrock had to be a priority for him until he got it off the ground, but he was going to have to go back to his obligations in Dallas soon. He'd find good people to run Bedrock, too, he was sure. He just hadn't had a chance yet. For now, it was his…well, his baby. And he was enjoying the time he was spending with it too much to hand it over to someone else right now.

"That explains it, then," Shelby said.

It took him a minute to backtrack in their conversation, but he was still confused by her comment. "What explains what?"

She gestured around the penthouse. "Why there are no personal touches."

"What do you mean?" He thought there were plenty of personal touches. Even though the decor wasn't exactly inspiring, he thought the decorator had done a pretty good job with all the throw pillows and artwork and stuff.

"I mean, anyone could live here," Shelby said. "It doesn't really scream 'Cameron Waite.' It doesn't scream anything, to be frank. But it's nice," she hurried to say again, as if she thought he might be insulted by her comments.

Which he wasn't. Hell, hadn't he been thinking the same thing yesterday? There really wasn't much of him here. Which maybe was why, every time he came home, it didn't feel like he was, you know, coming home. It felt more like going back to a hotel room. He hadn't bothered to bring anything to Emerald Ridge from his place in Dallas, nor had he acquired anything personal since coming here. Then again, there wasn't much of him at the house in Dallas, either, since his parents had been the ones to decorate that over the years. It was a beautiful house. It just wasn't his house. Certainly it didn't, as Shelby said, scream "Cameron Waite" any more than his penthouse here did.

Then again, his penthouse here felt a lot more welcoming with Shelby in it. It was just homier somehow with her here. She had that kind of presence in a place, he guessed. Some people were like that.

"Lunch first," he said as he made his way to the kitchen. "Then you can tell me what's brought you out and about."

She took a seat on one of the stools at his breakfast bar as he went to the fridge for sandwich fixings. When he withdrew and held up a bottle of water for her approval, she nodded, so he withdrew a glass from the cabinet, splashed in the contents and set it before her. They made the usual chitchat as Cameron made lunch, about how pleasantly mild the weather had been for the past week, about the new prickly pear kolaches Emerald Ridge Bakery just rolled out, about the high school raffling off a brand-spanking-new PlayStation, about—

"My father died this morning."

Shelby dropped that bit of information just as Cameron set their plates with their sandwiches on the breakfast bar in front of her and took his seat on the stool beside hers. And from the way she said it, she might as well have just told him she'd put a hole in her favorite pair of socks.

Sure he misunderstood, he said, "I'm sorry, what?"

She looked at the sandwich, then at him. "My father died this morning," she repeated.

Okay, he'd definitely heard correctly. "Shelby, I'm so sorry. I had no idea."

She thanked him for his condolences then tried to explain the morning's events in a way that made sense. But what came out instead ended up being kind of a stream of conscious rambling about anything *but* the morning's events. Probably because she was nowhere closer to making sense of things now than she'd been when she first heard the news. She seemed to realize that, too, eventually, right around the time she was saying something about never making close friends at boarding school because of going back and forth all year long, and classmates sometimes not returning from one year to the next, because she aburptly stopped speaking and covered her mouth with her hand.

Cameron was beginning to understand that this must be the way she dealt with stress and anxiety, by saying whatever popped into her head—and a *lot* must pop into her head when she was stressed and anxious—only to stop and regret it once she realized what she was doing.

She dropped her hand but closed her eyes. "I'm sorry," she said. "I didn't mean to dump a verbal mess into your lap again."

"It's not a mess," Cameron assured her. "It's totally understandable. You've had a shock to your system. I'm amazed you're handling it as well as you are. A lot of people would be a huge, sobbing wreck."

She opened her eyes again. "I don't feel like I'm handling it at all. To be honest, I'm not sure I've even accepted yet that he's gone. I should be a basket case, but..." She looked stricken. "I just don't feel...anything. Not grief. Not fear. Not loss. I'm beginning to realize that it's not that I didn't know my father all that well. It's that I didn't know my father in any way, shape, or form. Yes, he did his best when he was home, but... I have so few memories of him being a dad to us." She released a shaky breath, visibly fighting to keep her composure before going on. "If you asked me the most basic questions about him—his favorite color or food or what kind of music he liked—I couldn't tell you. In so many ways, he was a stranger to me. To my whole family. I just don't know what to feel right now, Cameron."

He scooted his stool closer to hers and nudged her plate gently, but meaningfully toward her. "Eat," he said simply. "Putting something in your stomach will help clear your thoughts. I know how it is to lose someone the way you have. A father's death, especially, can leave a big hole in your life, no matter what your relationship with him was. Even if we're not close to them, even if we don't see them as much as we'd like, for most people, fathers represent authority and make the rules and keep chaos at bay. After they're gone, we start wondering how we're supposed to keep everything together without them. That was their job, not ours."

Shelby thought about that for a moment, then nodded. "I forgot you said you lost your folks, too. I'm sorry."

"Thanks. It's okay. From what you've said, it sounds like my dad was around for me a lot more than yours was for you. Before his death, I would have told you he and I were pretty close. But after he passed, I realized…"

"What?" she asked when he didn't finish.

Cameron sighed. "I realized that even though he was active in my life, *he* never really knew *me*. Not the way a father who spends that much time with his kid should know them."

"But—"

"Eat," he said again. "We're not here to talk about me. You need to put something in your stomach. For you and Spud both."

She smiled a little at his use of her baby's nickname. Then, dutifully, she lifted the sandwich and took a small bite, chewing slowly, then swallowing. Then she took another. And another. Cameron joined her, and for a few minutes, they only sat in companionable silence side by side. When Shelby was about halfway through, she lifted her water to take a sip.

When she put it back down, he asked, "How did you find out? I thought he was supposed to be out of town until tomorrow?"

She lifted her sandwich again, then seemed to lose her appetite and put it back on the plate to fiddle with her napkin instead. "His attorney, Hamish Inland, came to the house this morning with Chief Campbell to tell us. I'm still not sure why someone up in New York called Daddy's attorney instead of his wife, but there it is. Mr. Inland came to Emerald Ridge to tell us as soon as he heard. Daddy had a heart attack during the night in his hotel room and was found this morning. Mr. Inland is taking care of the details. That's all we know for now."

That was enough to know, he thought. Even with details, hearing about the death of a loved one made a person feel hazy and indistinct.

"But as bad as it was to learn about Daddy's death," Shelby continued, "there was something else we learned about him this morning that was almost even worse."

What could possibly be worse than finding out your father died? Cameron wondered. Before he could ask, though, Shelby told him.

"Mama and Jillian and I weren't his only family."

He hoped by that she meant her father was married to his business. The way his own father had been. Hell, the way he was himself.

Until she added, "He married two other women after he married my mother. And he had children with those women."

Guess not.

"Not only that," she went on before he had a chance to comment—not that he had any idea how to respond to a revelation like that—"but he had a mistress, too, right here in Emerald Ridge, while he was married to all three of them. And there's reason to believe he had *another* child with her. Which means I have at least three half siblings that I never knew about before this morning. Probably four."

She looked at him expectantly. But all he could say was, "Whoa."

It wasn't exactly the pithiest response, Cameron knew. But it was the only thing he could think in that moment. It was the same reaction he'd had when he first discovered Drake's existence and that he had a twin brother he'd never known about. Shelby had three, maybe four, siblings she was only finding out about. That was like *Whoa* quadrupled.

"Yeah," she said with much understatement.

Cameron listened with a mixture of awe and disbelief as Shelby recounted, more rationally this time, what she, her sister and mother had learned from her father's attorney that morning. Then shared what she had discovered about her other families in the dossier he gave them to review afterward, which was what she had been poring over while she waited for him to come home. Admittedly, she still didn't have a lot of details about the wheres and whyfores of her father's actions, but wow, what a story.

Archibald Fortune had married not one, but two women, both within a year of his first marriage to Shelby's mother, then proceeded to start families with all three of them. One of his children, a son, was older than Shelby was. Although Archibald had married her mother first, she wasn't the oldest of the heirs. That had to exacerbate the confusion and hurt even more. To be thinking all this time that you had the specialness of being your father's firstborn, only to discover that no, you were second fiddle.

"The dossiers Mr. Inland gave us mostly just had name, rank and serial number type stuff," she continued. "My older brother, Penn, has a brother named Hayes who's the same age as Jillian. And Daddy's other wife has a daughter, Madeline, who's younger than the rest of us, something Jillian is probably coming to terms with, since she's not the baby anymore." She expelled an incredulous sound. "Listen to me, talking like we're one big happy family who vacationed together every summer and spent every Christmas morning opening presents under the tree when none of us has even met yet."

"And the other families are in Dallas and Houston?" Cameron asked, echoing another fact she mentioned.

She nodded. "Born and raised."

"I can't believe no one ever knew about this before now. I mean Dallas is only an hour away from Emerald Ridge. And Houston is only a few hours from Dallas. It's unfathomable that none of you figured it out before now. Living so close to each other and having the kind of father you all have?" He shook his head in disbelief. "I mean, it's not like Archibald Fortune was some nobody who could keep three families under wraps. His name was in the financial section of all the big papers on a fairly regular basis. He must have had some pretty major professional *and* social obligations. How did they never overlap?"

"Right?" Shelby said. "I know Texas is a big state, but still. Daddy was always super careful about making sure our names and photos weren't included in any articles written about him. We always thought it was to protect our privacy, and maybe it was to a degree, but it makes way more sense now. And he and Mama always limited on our social media use when we were growing up. Again, I assumed that was for our protection, but now I can't help thinking he had selfish reasons for that, too."

Cameron nodded. "It's still a lot to keep under wraps."

"It is," Shelby agreed. "I think about all the shindigs Daddy and Mama went to when we were kids—art galas, sports events, political fundraisers… How on earth could she have not run into at least one of his other wives at one of those things? And Jillian and I both competed in school stuff all over the state before we went to boarding school, and all us siblings are close in age. For all I know, some of us were at the same events and never even realized it. Yeah, there are a lot of Fortunes all over Texas, but the mind does boggle."

Cameron shook his head again. The mind really did boggle. A hundred years ago, it was probably pretty easy to hide multiple marriages and families. But in this day and age of the internet and social media, where it was pretty much impossible to hide anything? Archibald Fortune must have had some pretty major IT pros on his payroll to keep his comings and goings—and that of his three families—scrubbed or hidden from sight online. And he must have paid them a ton for both their knowledge and their discretion.

"I'll find out more tomorrow," Shelby said. "All three families are meeting at Emerald Ridge Hotel for a reading of my father's will. We'll all be under the same roof, at the same time, for the first time in our lives."

Wow, talk about a recipe for disaster. "And your father's lawyer thinks this is a good idea?"

"Lawyers," she corrected him. "Daddy had one for each family, evidently. Brothers, at that. Triplet brothers."

"So all three of them knew about all this stuff when none of the families did?"

"Looks that way. And yeah, all of us meeting together for the reading of the will is probably not a good idea. But it's what my father wanted, so that's what's going to happen. Barely twenty-four hours to process everything and prepare."

"You know, if you weren't pregnant, I'd say we should open a bottle of bourbon right about now."

She laughed at that. "Hold that thought. I'm sure the repercussions of this are going to last a good, long time." Her expression suddenly changed, and she cried, "Oh, my God, I didn't thank you for the gift basket from Lone Star Little Ones you sent! Cameron, I am so sorry! It arrived this morning. That was so thoughtful of you."

"Considering the kind of morning you've had, I'm not surprised it slipped your mind. I didn't even remember it myself until you said that."

"It was beautiful," she told him. "And so kind of you. Thank you."

"You're welcome."

"Even if it did sorta put me on the spot with my mother and sister."

She made the same kind of face at him that a toddler would give a bowl of broccoli, then smile. He was happy she was coming out of her funk, and that he was somehow instrumental in being a part of that, even if it meant being reduced to a bowl of broccoli.

"You still haven't told them about Spud?" he asked.

She shook her head. "Mama got the call from Mr. Inland before I woke up, and I could tell from the minute I saw her when I came downstairs that there was something wrong, so I didn't bring it up. Then, after Mr. Inland told us about Daddy… It just would have been too much for one morning. You continue to be the only one I've told about it."

Cameron still wasn't sure how to feel about that. On one hand, it pleased him enormously—probably more than it should—that Shelby Fortune had picked him to be first to hear news of what must be the biggest event in her life to date. But on the other hand… Even if she wasn't as close to her family as other people were, or hadn't had the chance to tell them yet, didn't she have friends who would be more appropriate vessels for that kind of announcement?

Then again, hadn't she just divulged to him in her anxious rambling how she didn't have those kinds of friendships? Ironic how being shipped off to boarding school at a young age and forced into constant contact with others had actually had the opposite effect on her socialization. And as much as she defended and seemed to love the pageant circuit, he guessed it could be rough to make close connections with people who were, essentially, her competitors.

"I mean, yeah," she continued, "there were a few people in Dr. Chavez's office yesterday who were acquainted with me, but for all they knew, I was only there for my annual exam. Even with you sitting there, no one would have made the assumption I was pregnant, since you're not Dylan. So…" She dropped her hand to the soft curve of her belly, evident with the way she was sitting. "Just you and me and—"

And baby makes three, Cameron thought before he could stop himself.

"—and Dr. Chavez," she finished.

Oh, right. The doctor. That's what she was talking about. No way did he and Shelby and her baby add up to anything.

"And the sonographer," she seemed to remember then. "And maybe some others in the office. But I'm sure there's some kind of HIPAA thing in place that's kept them all from saying anything."

"So when do you think you'll be able to tell your family?" he asked.

She muttered a derisive sound. "Which one? I have three. Maybe four."

It heartened him more that she could keep her sense of humor amid everything that was happening to her. Softly, he told her, "The one that means the most to you."

For some reason, the look that came over her face then was that none of those families meant as much to her as present company did. Again, Cameron was hit by a wave of something he knew he had no business feeling. But he couldn't help it. There was just something about Shelby that made him feel things he'd never felt before. And hell, if he was feeling this way after only knowing her a couple of days… But that was what was so weird. He didn't feel like he'd only known her a couple of days. He felt like the two of them had known each other forever.

He honestly didn't realize how close the two of them were sitting until she suddenly leaned toward him and pressed her mouth against his. It was a brief, chaste kiss, and when she pulled away again, she looked as surprised as he was. Instead of retreating, though—or apologizing or trying to brush it off as inconsequential—she leaned in and kissed him again. And this time, it wasn't quick. It wasn't particularly chaste, either. This time, when Shelby kissed Cameron, it was with intention, with purpose and with affection. She brushed her lips lightly over his—once, twice, three times—then covered his mouth completely with hers. And unable to help himself—okay, maybe not *wanting* to help himself—Cameron kissed her back.

As they lost themselves to the kiss, he reached for her, curving one hand over her shoulder and the other over her hip. Shelby cupped his jaw and splayed her other palm over his chest, their lips moving in sync. After that, he wasn't sure how much time passed. All Cameron knew was that he and Shelby were close and intimate, and it felt really good, and that something inside him was growing warm and wistful in a way he'd never felt before.

And then, suddenly, she was pulling away, removing her hands from him to cover her mouth with both, just like she did when her words got away from her. Except that this time it wasn't words she'd lost control of. This time it was herself.

"I am so sorry," she said quietly from behind her fingers. "I don't know what made me do that."

Cameron wanted to tell her he didn't care what made her do that, and he wasn't sorry at all, and, in fact, they could do it again if she wanted. Then he reminded himself she was in a vulnerable position emotionally, and the last thing he should be doing was taking advantage of that. Not that he thought he'd taken advantage by kissing her back. But if he pressed her for more now, he sure as hell would be.

"You don't have to apologize," he told her, his voice coming out low and husky. "Sometimes people behave in surprising ways to situations that are..." He blew out an errant breath. "Out of the ordinary. You had a shock to your system this morning, Shelby. Lot of emotions inside there swirling around. I'm the one who should apologize for not stopping things before they got out of hand."

She smiled softly at that. "Is it terrible that I'm kinda glad you didn't? I think I needed that."

He grinned back. "Yeah, well, I'm certainly not going to complain. But we should probably make sure it doesn't happen again."

At least not until after she got her life straightened out, he couldn't help adding to himself. Then again, with a baby on the way, it could be a couple of decades before that happened. Probably best if he just put all thoughts of *anything* happening with Shelby Fortune, other than friendship, right out of his head.

Even if she wasn't pregnant, and even if she hadn't just lost her father and discovered his deceit, they were both coming off recent breakups that had left them feeling hurt and betrayed. He was still working through discovering a brother he never knew he had. They both needed to get their lives and themselves on track before either one of them could even think about moving beyond friendship.

She nodded. "You're right. I guess I'm wound pretty tight right now."

"Completely understandable," he told her. "And if you ever need to talk, I'll be happy to be your sounding board."

He hoped he made clear that that was all he would be. But judging by the nod of determination she gave him, he was pretty sure she understood.

"Now finish your sandwich," he told her.

Because, honestly, in that moment, he had no idea what else to say. Let alone think or feel. Shelby Fortune wasn't the only one who was wound too tight just then. Cameron was, as well. Because as much as he knew the kiss they just shared was a mistake, there was a not-so-little part of him that felt like it was the first thing to go right in his life in a long time.

She smiled as she picked up her sandwich and did just that. Cameron followed suit, grateful they had something to do with their mouths that would keep conversation—and kissing—to a minimum. He just wished there was something that would give his brain the same diversion. Because it was going to be a while before he stopped thinking about the way Shelby's lips felt against his. How warm her skin was beneath the fabric of her dress. And how good it felt to have her hand cupping his cheek and her fingers open over his heart…

Chapter Six

Like other luxury lodgings of its kind, Emerald Ridge Hotel was an ode to serenity, with its muted colors and chic fixtures and elegant touches meant to put weary travelers at ease and make them feel as if they were immersed in a world of refinement. Lots of marble and mahogany and velvet. Usually, Shelby loved coming here, because she truly did feel like a pampered princess when she did. This morning, not so much. She barely registered the place. As she, Jillian and their mother made their way across the lobby, they did so in silence, all of them still reeling from yesterday's news and apprehensive about what awaited them at the meeting that was mere minutes away. She was reasonably sure that all three of them continued to be in some state of shock.

Then again, Shelby was still reeling from her kiss with Cameron yesterday, too. And she still wasn't sure what had sparked it. There had just been something about the way he advised her to share the news of her pregnancy to the family that mattered to her most. After he said that, she'd found herself wondering what really constituted family, anyway. For all intents and purposes, she had three of them now. And the man she'd always thought of as her father felt kind of like a stranger. In that moment,

Cameron had almost felt as much like family as anyone did. And that had her reeling, too.

She expelled a restless breath as she and her family—the one she was born to—made their way to the room Mr. Inland had reserved for them. Truth be told, she didn't know what Cameron felt like. She only knew being with him felt good. Everything was still so jumbled in her head this morning. And in her heart. A few weeks ago, she'd been living her life the way she did every day—well-planned, upbeat, free of strife or surprise. Now, suddenly, everything was different. *She* was different. In spite of her planning and list-making and absolute certainty that her life was totally on track, everything had changed. And she was beginning to think that nothing would ever get it back to where it used to be.

One thing at a time, Shelby, she told herself. *Just get through this morning, and then you can work on what comes next.*

Although she almost always knew what to wear for any occasion, she'd been at a complete loss as to what was appropriate for the one of *Meeting Your Deceased Father's Secret Families*. So she had thrown on the first thing she pulled out of her closet—a pale lavender sheath dress. Over that, she'd donned a creamy cardigan with a beaded neckline. Jillian had stayed true to her tailored ways in dark chocolate trousers and an amber shirt that brought out the warm hue of her hazel eyes. Their mother, who normally strove to be the fashion centerpiece of any event she attended, was in a black shirtwaist befitting a grieving widow, her only accessories a pearl necklace and earrings, her dark hair tucked into a chignon at her nape. This despite the fact that there would be two other widows in attendance who would probably be wearing nearly the same thing, the biggest faux pas Agatha Fortune could step into. Oh, the horrors.

Stop it, Shelby, she told herself. This was not the time for sarcasm. Even if it was the way she tended to deal with stressful situations. As long as she did it in silence, she figured she was okay. Today, though, even silent derision seemed out of place.

They followed the directions Mr. Inland had texted them until they located the José Antonio Lavarro room, a boxy conference room with folded-up tables pushed to one side and two walls made of dividers. Three short rows of chairs were neatly positioned in the center of the room in front of a table with a dais and some other seating behind it. The setting was as far removed as it could be from a Gothic mansion on a stormy night, but Shelby couldn't quite shake the idea that they were all waiting for a tuxedoed butler to usher in a deerstalker-wearing detective who said, "I guess you're all wondering why I called you here tonight."

The Emerald Ridge Fortunes weren't the first on-scene, Shelby noted the minute they entered, as there were two other people in the opposite corner from the entry, mingling with Mr. Inland and his two identical triplet brothers. One was a woman who looked to be about the same age as Agatha, with long red hair and, yes, a black dress and understated pearls, though her neckline was a less conservative scooped one. With her was a man close to Shelby and Jillian in age who, she couldn't help thinking, bore a strong resemblance to their father. He was tall, like Archibald had been, with dark hair and eyes. Judging by the way he was cradling the Stetson in his hand, she was going to guess he was Hayes Fortune who, according to the dossier, was a former champion bronc rider and now ran a string of rodeo camps for kids. Which meant the woman with him was Damaris Fortune, Archibald's second wife, since she was the only one who had given him sons.

Shelby was assailed again by the realization that all those years when she'd wondered as a girl if her father might have liked to have a boy child in addition to his daughters, he actually had two of them. One of whom had been born before she was. *Gee, Daddy, you really didn't waste any time on that, did you?*

Stop it, she told herself again. These people weren't her enemy. The Houston Fortunes had been as much in the dark about Archibald's deceit as the Emerald Ridge Fortunes—and the Dallas Fortunes, for that matter—had been. Her half siblings and their mothers were as much victims of their father as she and Jillian and her mother were.

She tried to take some small comfort in reminding herself that her mother had been her father's first wife—his only *legal* wife—meaning her half siblings weren't rightful heirs the way she and her sister were. But in this day and age, birth in or out of wedlock didn't hold much social distinction and probably didn't even have the same legal protections it had once upon time.

But even telling herself that she and Jillian and her mother were the "legitimate" ones gave Shelby little reassurance. The women's marital status with regard to Archibald was of no more consequence than birth order was. Each and every one of her father's heirs had been cheated out of a real childhood with the man who had donated half of their DNA. Not to mention that all of their mothers had been cheated out of an authentic marriage to him. Bottom line? All of the Fortunes in the room that morning were, in a sense, illegitimate. They all shared that, at least, in common.

Oh, yay.

Before Shelby's thoughts could get too maudlin, the other Fortunes glanced at the newcomers and gave them a quick once-over. Then they seemed to move even farther away than they already were, tucking themselves more resolutely into their corner. Instinctively of one mind, Shelby and her sister and mother did likewise, heading into the corner opposite them, creating even more distance.

Like boxers sizing up their opponent, Shelby couldn't help thinking. Already, the antagonism was setting in. And that was the last thing any of them should be feeling. As if they were enemies. But they weren't. All of them had to remember that.

Hamish Inland lifted a hand to Shelby and her family, then said something to the others and broke away from the group to approach.

"I hope you were all able to get at least a little sleep last night," he said quietly to all three.

Yeah, right. Between mulling yesterday's news and replaying Cameron Waite's kiss, Shelby had barely closed her eyes last night. And today was promising even more turmoil. She wasn't sure she'd ever sleep again.

Agatha shook her head. "I appreciate the thought, Hamish, but I just want to get this over with."

"I understand," he told her. "We're just waiting for the Dallas Fortunes to arrive, and then we can begin."

As if conjured by the statement, two more people wandered into the room to join the others. The first, a woman who looked a decade younger than Agatha, entered confidently, almost fiercely, as if she couldn't wait to get this show on the road. The third widow, Shelby quickly deduced. Taffy Fortune. But, wow, was she clearly *not* in mourning.

On the contrary, her dress was flaming red, and where the other Mrs. Fortunes had their hair arranged in a way befitting a time of sorrow, this Mrs. Fortune's was expertly, and—Shelby could tell with her pageant experience—quite recently styled and balayaged by an absolute expert at both. Her makeup, too, was perfect, as was her manicure. She wore a dazzling string of diamonds around her neck and wrist that sparked even brighter under the hotel fluorescents, as if she wanted to make a statement—that statement being *I am just as important as the rest of you, maybe even more so.*

Behind her was her daughter, Madeline, the same age as Jillian at twenty-eight, and an event planner by trade. Her long red hair was caught at her nape in a loose ponytail, and her attire was what Shelby had always thought of as professional beige, from her trousers to her blazer to the shell she wore beneath it. It made it difficult for her to form an opinion about her half sister one way or another.

True to his word, the dossiers Mr. Inland had given them hadn't revealed much about her father's other families other than their names, ages, locales and jobs. Shelby had googled each of them after reading over the information but hadn't learned much more than she already knew. She'd wondered briefly what the dossiers on her and Jillian and Agatha had contained, then realized she didn't much care. Which was a strange thing for her to realize. Competing in pageants meant *always* caring what other people thought about her. In spite of her assurances to Cameron that pageant life involved a lot more than just looking good, her appearance—more to the point, her *image*—had always had to be first and foremost in her mind. When one's entire professional future depended on being judged by strangers, it was impossible not to worry about what others thought. Today, though…

Today Shelby realized she didn't give one red-hot patootie what anyone thought about her. She wasn't sure when that change had happened. Or why. She only knew there were far more important things for her to be concerned about now. Her baby, most of all, but her mother and sister, too. Even before learning about her father's death and her newly discovered extended family, Shelby had begun to understand that there were infinitely more important things in the world than winning the approval of others. Maybe that was why, after hearing the judges' comments at her last pageant, she hadn't felt mortified or embarrassed. She'd felt *mad*. Mad that people could be so shallow as to judge others on their appearance, of all things, when even the most upright, forthright, do-right appearances could hide all kinds of ugliness, malice and deceit. Image didn't matter. Actions and human decency did. All Shelby knew was that she refused to be a slave to her image anymore.

In fact, she decided on the spot that once she got her coaching business up and running—and the more she thought about it now, the more she began to think this was a fortuitous time to start getting that in order—that would to be the focus of her mentoring. Ensuring that everyone she worked with understood that what really mattered was the integrity and passion they brought to their pageant efforts, not the opinion of strangers. On how they could change the whole world if they wanted to, by staying true to the things that mattered most. Kindness and respect and decency.

"Ah, I see everyone has arrived now," Mr. Inland said. "If I could have you all join me to be seated."

Jillian looked around the room again. "Wait, I thought there were supposed to be two half brothers. Where's the other one?"

Mr. Inland looked a little uncomfortable. "I'm afraid Damaris said that her son, Penn, would not be able to make the meeting today."

"I thought we all had to be here for the reading of the will," Shelby said.

"Although your father requested that everyone be present this morning," the attorney replied, "the reading of the will is a formality. The terms, however, are iron-clad." Before any of them could object further, he extended a hand toward the chairs set up in the center of the room and said, "If you'll come this way."

Shelby noticed that the other attorneys had joined their respective families and were guiding them in that direction, as well. Belatedly, everyone in the room seemed to realize what a bad idea it had been to put the chairs so close together, as all of them hesitated before sitting, no one wanting to get any closer than they had to. The three attorneys also seemed to realize their mistake too late and hastily corralled everyone into whatever chair was closest. Shelby found herself sitting next to her half brother Hayes, something that roused all the irrational resentment about him being the son she suspected her father always wanted.

Even so, what was left of the pageant queen inside her forced her to be pleasant. “Hello,” she said softly when they were both settled. “I'm Shelby.”

To his credit, he smiled, something that put her a little more at ease. “I'm Hayes,” he said. As an afterthought, he extended his hand toward her.

Automatically, Shelby took it, then introduced him to her mother, seated on her other side, and Jillian, who sat beside Agatha. Both nodded and greeted him as politely as they could, then turned their attention back to the three attorneys, who had moved behind the table. Hamish Inland took his place at the dais, while his brothers, Carlton and Hans, folded themselves into chairs on each side of him. Shelby looked around at her companions long enough to realize that her father's widows were staunchly avoiding meeting one another's eyes, while the half siblings seemed unable to look away from each other. Somehow, they all managed to throw each other a weak smile and even murmur a few soft hellos. Mostly, though, everyone in the room, including the Inlands, seemed more than a little uncomfortable.

“I wish we were all meeting under better circumstances,” Mr. Inland began.

Before he could say more, Taffy Fortune, Archibald's third wife, barked out a sound of derision. “I wish we weren't meeting at all,” she said crisply.

“Taffy, please,” Hans Inland said. At least, Shelby was pretty sure it was Hans. Although all three brothers looked exactly alike, she remembered from the dossier that Hans was the one representing that branch of the family.

"Fine," Taffy said. "I'll be a good girl." But she punctuated the statement with a scornful expulsion of breath that suggested she would be anything but.

Her daughter, Madeline, Shelby couldn't help noticing, threw the others an apologetic look, but covered her mother's arm with an affectionate hand that indicated the two were close.

The Mr. Inland representing Shelby's family cleared his throat, straightened his glasses and said, "Let's begin, shall we?"

Shelby's mother reached for her hand and wove their fingers together, then took Jillian's with her other, as if wanting to make clear that the three Emerald Ridge Fortunes were a unit. Mr. Inland thanked the three families for coming, expressed his condolences to all involved and assured them they would all receive a copy of the will before they parted ways. Then he began to read. Shelby did her best to focus on all the legalese, but most of it seemed to be pretty standard stuff. The gist of it was that Archibald's estate would be divided equally among his heirs, blah blah blah. Then the lawyer got to the part where her father stated that he did not want a funeral, nor to be traditionally buried, but wanted to be cremated instead, his ashes scattered in Emerald Ridge River. Not by any members of his family, however. Only by his attorneys.

Shelby had no idea how to interpret that last part of the announcement. Her mother, especially, seemed to find the revelation distressing. "But Archibald and I bought plots in the cemetery at Hopewell Church," she said. "We did it right after we married. So that we'd be side by side. He said 'till death do us part' wasn't good enough. He wanted us to be together forever."

Damaris Fortune also seemed puzzled by the news—at least part of it. "I knew he wanted to be cremated," she said, "but he told me he wanted his ashes scattered in Galveston Bay." When everyone turned to look at her, she explained, "Every year on our anniversary—the ones where Archibald was home, I mean—he took me for a cruise on the FantaSea yacht."

Shelby's mother's fingers clenched tightly around hers, and she bit back a strangled sound. Shelby knew what she was thinking. That their father had almost never been home for his anniversaries with her, even though he always sent a huge bouquet of roses.

"Well, I couldn't care one way or another," Taffy Fortune piped up. "I wouldn't go to that rat bastard's funeral anyway."

"*Mother*," Madeline said from beside her. "You promised."

"Yeah, well, promises were made to be broken. Just ask your father."

No one said a word in response to that. Even the Inland brothers seemed to have no idea how to react. Shelby would give her father's third wife props for not being afraid to speak the truth, even if maybe now wasn't an ideal time for it.

"Archibald was quite clear in his request," Mr. Inland continued. "He had fond memories of Emerald Ridge River from when he was young, when he would catch bass and crawfish there to feed himself as a teenager, after his parents passed away. It was a place of hope for him."

"He never told me that," Shelby's mother muttered under her breath. "And I thought I knew him so well."

Damaris, who was seated immediately in front of Agatha, turned in her seat. "He never told me that, either," she said quietly. "And I thought I knew him, too."

Shelby listened for any sign of anguish from the other woman, but Damaris was stone-faced and matter-of-fact. As she turned back around in her chair, Shelby noted that Taffy, who was sitting a few chairs down from Damaris and had also obviously heard her mother's comment, only rolled her eyes dramatically. Looked like her mother might be the widow who was grieving most for the man who had lied to all of them. As if to illustrate that, Agatha began to cry in earnest, releasing her daughters' hands to retrieve a tissue from her purse.

The attorney continued to read the will, listing the assets that were to be divided and in which ways. "However," he added as he turned a page. He looked up at each of the heirs, eyeing them one by one. "There is one stipulation, and it's a rather significant one."

Shelby sighed softly. Of course there was a stipulation. How did a man divide his estate between not one, not two but three families he'd created without there being stipulations. She was just surprised that there was only one, even if it was *significant*.

"As you were all informed yesterday, there is reason to believe Archibald had a sixth heir by a woman here in Emerald Ridge. Lianna Dunhill, with whom he had an affair thirty years ago."

In all the turmoil of the last twenty-four hours, Shelby had honestly almost forgotten that her father's affair had happened here in Emerald Ridge, right under her mother's nose. He truly had been a stranger to all of them. Her mother most of all.

"Unfortunately," Mr. Inland continued, "at this point, although we do know from Archibald that his mistress was at one point pregnant, we do not know if she ever actually had a child or if that child survived to adulthood. He wanted very much to know for sure but he wasn't able to discover it before he died. If this child, now adult, does exist, Archibald was adamant they be considered as much an heir as the rest of his children."

When it looked as if the rest of Archibald's children were about to object, the lawyer hurried on, "This heir will *not* be sharing equally in Archibald's estate. He had a specific bequest for this heir, should they be found. A plot of land on the outskirts of Emerald Ridge that has been in his family for generations."

"Land?" Jillian said. "What land?"

Shelby nodded. "Yeah, Daddy only had Fortune and Daughters Ranch here. We never heard a thing about another property."

"I know what land Hamish is talking about," Agatha said quietly. "Archibald had it when we married and didn't want to let it go because it was the only thing his family ever had. He was adamant about it never being developed, but he refused to sell it. He never said why. I always thought maybe he was planning to divide it into two tracts and give one to each of you girls as a wedding present or something." She shrugged. "It's a mystery, really. But it was his land. His choice."

"It wasn't worth much when the two of you married," Mr. Inland told Agatha. "Now, however, it is worth millions. It is also the key to who Archibald truly was. At least that's what he's always said of that property."

At this, every Fortune in the room turned to look at the attorney. But only Taffy spoke. "The key to who he truly was? What the hell is that supposed to mean? Seems pretty clear who Archibald truly was. A lying snake."

"Mother," Madeline said in the same cautious way she had before. But again, her tone and posture suggested she felt more sympathy toward her mother than she did derision.

"Oh, please, Madeline," her mother replied. Though her timbre when speaking to her daughter was gentler. "I always knew your father was cheating on me. I just figured he had mistresses, not other wives."

"I know things weren't great between you and Dad," Madeline said. "But this isn't the time or place to get into any of that."

Taffy expelled another disgusted sound. "Whatever."

"This land," Mr. Inland continued as if none of them had spoken, "will, as I said, be the sole bequest to your missing half sibling. According to Archibald, there is something on that land that will make clear how his life became what it was, and answer any questions you all may have about how and why he did what he did and lived the way he lived." He cleared his throat. "But in order to find the key that will unlock all that, the five half siblings—including Penn Fortune, who isn't present today—must work together to track down Lianna Dunhill's child. You must also locate your missing half sibling in order to inherit your own shares of your father's estate. If the missing heir is not found, or if you do not uncover irrefutable evidence that the child never existed, then no one will receive an inheritance, and Archibald's estate will be divided among the charities listed below."

As Shelby's head began to spin at what Hamish Inland was saying, he began to read off a list of organizations, most of which she'd never even heard her father mention. As confused as she'd been yesterday by everything the attorney had told them, she was even more confounded now. As if it weren't bad enough that her father had bamboozled nearly a dozen people sitting in this room, now he was trying to control them from the grave. How were five people, who were complete strangers in spite of their shared blood, supposed to find a sixth person who might not even exist? The Inland brothers must have every avenue at their disposal to find a missing person, and they obviously hadn't been able to do it. How could Archibald think his surviving children would have better luck?

Unless maybe he'd asked the attorneys to *not* look for the missing heir specifically because he *did* want his surviving children to be the ones who searched for them?

Oh, Daddy, how could you?

Mr. Inland was still speaking, now outlining exactly how Archibald's children were expected to go about their task. He reiterated that the half siblings would be required to work together to find the missing heir in order to inherit their portion of his estate, though not via email or social media or text. They had to find this heir *in person.* Furthermore, they would regularly report back to the three attorney brothers, who had been Archibald's trusted lawyers for more than forty years. To that end, the children must submit regular detailed reports of *how* they were working together to achieve their goal. As in they were going to have to stay in constant contact with each other here in Emerald Ridge until they found their missing half brother or sister.

At this, the four half siblings present all turned to look at each other, clearly sizing each other up to see how readily any of them could undertake such a task. Judging by their expressions, which Shelby was reasonably certain mirrored her own, none of them was especially confident in the variety of skill sets they had. She ticked off what she could remember from the dossiers Mr. Inland had given them. She was a former Miss Texas, and her sister was a horsey socialite. Madeline Fortune planned parties for a living. Hayes Fortune was an ex-rodeo champ and philanthropist. And his elusive brother, Penn, owned luxury hotels all over the world.

Oh, yeah. They were a real dream team when it came to solving a mystery. *Coming soon to Netflix!*

As if her thinking about Penn put the reminder into the attorney's head, too, he added, "And, Damaris, you need to make sure your son comes to Emerald Ridge as soon as possible. If he doesn't take part in this search with Hayes and Madeline and Shelby and Jillian, then that, too, will negate the terms of the will and make it impossible for any of them to inherit. Archibald was crystal clear. All five of his children must search for—and find—the sixth in order for anyone to inherit anything. Or they must prove beyond doubt that the sixth does not exist."

By this point, Shelby had gone from feeling confused to feeling numb. It was just too much to take in, too much to accept, too much to fathom. This time two days ago, she was sitting in the doctor's office talking to Cameron Waite, the most charming man she'd ever met, and she'd been about to discover whether she would be having a boy or a girl, and planning the way she would deliver the news to her mother and sister. She hadn't thought her life could possibly get more complicated than it already was. But by day's end, she'd been up to the challenge and had put a plan in place for how it would all go down.

Now, barely forty-eight hours later, she felt like her life was astride all four horses of the apocalypse, and they were all trying to head into different directions, and all she could do was hang on to their reins to keep them from running helter-skelter into chaos. She just had no idea what the future held now, for any of them.

She wasn't worried so much about the loss of the inheritance for herself. Between pageant prizes and endorsements and payments for personal appearances—and thanks to some great financial advice—Shelby knew she and little Spud would always be okay there. But she had no idea what kind of financial future awaited her sister, and her mother, for sure, would never make it without her husband's income and, now, inheritance. Although Mama had mentioned there was a life insurance policy, she'd also mentioned it wasn't a lot, since Archibald's estate was so enormous. If that estate now went away, Agatha was going to be in a precarious position. And if they lost the house, all of Shelby's dreams about raising little Spud in the place where she grew up herself would be crushed.

Hayes and his mother Damaris, Shelby noted, exchanged a somewhat chaotic look of their own, as if they were having similar thoughts. Before he said anything, though, his mother shook her head mutely, as if cautioning him the same way Madeline had Taffy Fortune a little while ago. Shelby glanced down at Jillian, only to find her sister looking more furious than she'd ever seen her before. Not that

Shelby blamed her. She was angry herself at the mess their father had created and left for them all to clean up. None of them had asked for their lives to be thrown into upheaval. But, wow, Archibald had sure made sure it would be their constant companion for a while.

Madeline Fortune, however, looked as pragmatic as her mother did acerbic. It was she who managed to quiet the others down.

"Look," she said, "I think I can say with some confidence that we four children of Archibald Fortune who are here today feel pretty much the same way right now. Angry, betrayed, confused."

Shelby was ready to go down the rest of the alphabet with things like *devastated, edgy, fretful…*

But Madeline continued, "Even if none of us really needs our father's inheritance to survive—though some of us might eventually, now that we've been shafted by our most recent employer, and hung out to dry by the one person we thought we could trust and—" She halted abruptly.

Wow, Shelby wondered what the story was there.

"Anyway," Madeline hurried on, "we should think of our mothers, who are also a big part of this. If nothing else, they deserve some kind of compensation for building their lives around a man they trusted who turned out to be anything but trustworthy."

At the mention of their mothers, the other siblings sobered. It was fairly clear none of them had been particularly close to their father. Not surprising, since he had doubtless been pretty much absent from all of their lives while they were growing up. But his wives had loved him on some level at some point, otherwise they never would have married him. Even Taffy Fortune, with her outbursts, must have loved Archibald in some way at some time. Otherwise, she wouldn't be so infuriated by him now.

Madeline was right. If nothing else, the children owed it to their mothers, who *had* been there for them while they were growing up, to do what they could to fulfill their father's last wish to locate his sixth child—their final half sibling. A half sibling who, if nothing else, also deserved to know the truth about their heritage and the fact that they had blood relations out there in the world.

"You're right, Madeline," Hayes said quietly. "I'll call my brother tonight and tell him he has to be a part of this whether he likes it or not, and to get his ass up here ASAP."

Whether he liked it or not? Shelby echoed to herself. Mr. Inland had just said Penn Fortune couldn't make it due to another obligation. Sounded more like he couldn't make it due to the fact that he just didn't *want* to make it.

Instead of saying anything about that, however—there would be plenty of time for the half siblings to compare notes and strategize later—she nodded.

"I agree," she said simply. "Count me in."

She looked at her sister. Jillian seemed as if she wanted to balk, but finally lifted a hand, palm out, as if in half surrender. "I agree, too," she said wearily. "I've never been a big fan of Dad, especially now, but Mama's been through enough. I'm in, too."

The three mothers, Shelby noticed, had been hanging on every word the siblings said, clearly finding comfort in Madeline's rationale and their children's agreement.

Hayes withdrew his phone from his pocket and punched in his code to unlock it. "I'll call Penn right now and see when he can get here."

Before doing that, though, he threw his mother another one of those curious glances that Shelby couldn't help thinking was a look of concern. Damaris, in return, looked a bit worried about something, but she nodded, and Hayes went back to his phone.

"He might even be able to catch a flight today," he said as he thumbed in his brother's number. "Or, hell, get in his car and drive."

Hayes spoke to his brother, the Inlands passed out a new dossier to each of the Fortunes, one they had prepared on Lianna Dunhill, their father's former mistress here in Emerald Ridge. Like the others—except for Hayes, who had left the group to speak to his brother and seemed to be doing so a bit contentiously at the moment—Shelby opened hers to see what kind of information was inside.

There wasn't much. A dated photo of a woman who was quite beautiful, along with her name and age, which at the time Archibald knew her, was twenty-four. Her last known address was an apartment above a long-gone riverside seafood restaurant called Duff's Catch, where she had worked as a waitress. Duff's had closed a decade ago, and the owners had relocated the business right here in the Emerald Ridge Hotel. It was now called Captain's, a swanky spot located on the penthouse level. They served five-star cuisine like blue-crab-stuffed lobster tails and Chilean sea bass with truffle vinaigrette. They'd come a long way from their fried catfish and hush puppies.

Oh, and there was also a section in the dossier that went into greater detail about how Lianna Dunhill had tried to blackmail their father. Turned out, she'd known Archibald was married when they started their affair—though not that he had more than one wife besides Agatha at the time—and had been adamant that he ask for a divorce so that he could marry her. When Archibald refused, Lianna dug more into his comings and goings and discovered he had other families. She did that the old-fashioned way, by following him around herself when she could and witnessing with her own eyes how he had two other homes and two other families occupying them. After that, she threatened to tell not just Archibald's other families about each other, but the press, too, unless he paid her *a lot* of money. Enough so that she could start a new life pretty much anywhere in the world, under whatever circumstances she wanted.

Just where are you, Lianna Dunhill? Shelby asked the photo paper-clipped to the Inlands' notes. She pulled out her own phone and did a quick search on the name. *No results found*, Google told her. Yeah, that would have been too easy. A young, pregnant woman from a small Texas town with a pocket full of blackmail cash really could have gone anywhere from here. Depending on how savvy Lianna was, she may have built an entirely new identity—an entirely new life—for herself anywhere in the country. Or anywhere on the planet. This wasn't going to be easy.

"So where do we start?" Jillian finally asked the room at large.

No one had a ready answer. And when Hayes finally returned to the group after ending his call to his brother, they realized there could be another snag.

"This might take some doing," he told them all. "I'm gonna have to fly to Houston and talk to Penn in person."

"Why? What's the problem?" Madeline asked.

Hayes hesitated, looked at his mother, who was talking to one of the Inlands on the other side of the room, then said matter-of-factly, "It's kind of complicated."

Well, that was the understatement of the century, Shelby thought.

"Look, my brother's a reasonable man," Hayes continued. "He'll come to his senses and understand how important this is after I talk to him some more. I *will* bring him back to Emerald Ridge with me. Tomorrow, if I can, but certainly before the end of the week. Let's all make plans to meet for dinner Friday night. Isn't there some kind of good seafood restaurant here in the hotel, up on the penthouse level or something?"

Shelby and Jillian chuckled at the question.

"What?" Hayes said.

Madeline looked just as confused. Of course they would be. Neither knew that Captain's was, in effect, Archibald's mistress's former employer.

"Lianna Dunhill used to work for the folks who own the restaurant upstairs," Shelby told him. "So yeah. I think Captain's is the perfect place for us all to meet. Seven o'clock Friday? I'll make a reservation for five on my way out."

"Sounds perfect," Madeline said. "In between now and then, we can all do some poking around to see what we can find out about Lianna Dunhill. If anything."

"Good luck." Standing, Taffy slung her purse over her shoulder. "I'm outta here. I trust y'all will play nice and not screw this up."

As Madeline shook her head at her mother's abrupt retreat, Hayes's mother, Damaris, rushed over to give him a quick hug. She said nothing, though, just threw him another one of those weird, knowing looks and bolted for the door. Shelby's mother was still seated, weeping softly into a tissue, a pile of others in her lap, where she'd dropped them.

Jillian sighed. "I'm gonna take Mama home," she said. "Make her a cup of pomegranate tea and see if she wants to watch *Romancing the Stone.* That usually cheers her up. We'll probably end up making it a day of marathon rom-coms. Want to join us?"

Shelby smiled. "Thanks. That actually sounds like a nice escape, but I think I need to be alone for a while. My brain is about to explode from all this stuff. Y'all have fun."

Jillian gave her a resigned smile, then went to collect their mother. Shelby watched as Hayes and Madeline made their way to the door and the Inland brothers collected their materials and did likewise. Hamish Inland stopped at the door when he realized Shelby was still in the room, then made his way back toward her.

"Is everything all right, Shelby?"

What a loaded question. A part of her was beginning to wonder if anything in her life would ever be right again. "It's fine," she told the attorney half-heartedly. "I'm just still a little stunned."

"You have every right to be," he assured her. He extended a hand toward the exit in a not-so-subtle indication that it was time to go. "Maybe a little fresh air will help you clear your head."

She nodded. A walk down Emerald Ridge Boulevard did sound kind of nice. She'd always loved the hustle and bustle of town and popping into and out of the string of boutiques and cafés.

As the two of them made their way to the exit, Mr. Inland told her, "My brothers and I will be in town for a few more days if you and your siblings need to speak to us any further."

"I'm sure we will," she said. "Thank you, and your brothers, for all you've done. I know Daddy couldn't have made this easy for any of you."

Mr. Inland stopped before they arrived at the door. "I know you and your family, all the families, must be experiencing a host of feelings for your father right now. But, Shelby, in spite of everything, Archibald Fortune was a good man. And he loved all of you very much. Please remember that."

She nodded but said nothing. She wasn't sure if she believed what the attorney said or not. Certainly, over the years, she recalled her father telling her and Jillian he loved them. He'd gone so far as to say they made him proud. And although he'd been absent from many of the events most fathers attended, he *had* been there for a couple of her life's biggest moments. He'd even flown in from God knew where to watch her compete the final night of the Miss America Pageant. And despite only coming in as third runner-up, he'd beamed as if she'd just become Empress of the Universe. Her rational mind, at least, knew he must have cared for her. Her heart, however…

Well. Her heart right now was every bit as scattered as her brain.

Chapter Seven

Cameron was the only customer at Lone Star Little Ones in downtown Emerald Ridge when the bell above the door jangled to announce another arrival. Thank God. As much as he appreciated how much help Flora Rodriguez, the owner, had given him, there was such a thing as *too much* help. He knew most people thought men were hopeless when it came to matters of all things baby-and-child-related, but he'd learned a lot since he'd created Bedrock. And he actually kind of enjoyed the hands-on parts like picking out supplies. Though he had to admit as he looked at the pile of merchandise Flora had placed behind the counter for him, she did seem to know her stuff when it came to what babies and new moms needed. Still, it was a relief to know she had another customer to focus on while he made a rundown of the rest of the shop.

He heard Flora greet the newcomer and glanced up to throw whoever it was a grateful smile, only to see Shelby Fortune stepping in from the bright sunlight outside. Inescapably, the memory of the kiss they shared the day before crowded his brain, and his pulse quickened. They'd somehow managed afterward to get themselves back on track conversation-wise and talk more about Shelby's newly discovered family and her fears about meeting them this morning. By the time she left his place, the kiss had pretty much been forgotten.

Well, okay, the kiss was probably something neither of them would forget for a while, but at least they'd each seemed to agree that it had just been one of those weird things that happened and would never happen again. Even so, Cameron wasn't sure what kind of reception he would receive from Shelby today. Especially since she must be here on the heels of meeting her newfound families. He wondered how that had gone, but considering the fact that she was out shopping alone instead of yakking it up over coffee with her new half siblings, he was going to go out on a limb and say the gathering hadn't ended with all of them being one big happy family.

She hadn't seen him yet, so he took a minute to observe her, marveling again at how beautiful she was, and how easily she responded to other people. Flora clearly liked her, judging by the friendly embrace the two women shared, and the way they launched into conversation as if they were old friends. Even though, Cameron knew, Flora hadn't lived in Emerald Ridge all that long. Shelby said something about just popping in for a quick look around, so the shop owner left her to her own devices after assuring her she was there if Shelby had any questions.

Oh, sure, the *pregnant woman* didn't need help picking stuff out for herself and her bun in the oven, but the guy who'd made his living in finance and didn't even have a womb needed all the help he could get? He actually laughed softly at the arrogance of his thoughts, a sound that made Shelby look in his direction. For the briefest of seconds, she looked a little panicked. Then she smiled. The same kind of smile she had that day at her doctor's office when he brought her a simple snack, and she looked like she'd be grateful forever.

"Hi, Cameron," she greeted him quietly, lifting her hand in a half wave.

"Hey, Shelby," he replied just as softly.

There was another moment of silence, as if neither of them knew what to do or say next. Which was weird, because, even after things got heated between them, they'd quickly returned to the same easy vibe they'd shared since the second they met. Okay, maybe they'd been a little *too* comfortable for a few moments when it came to the kiss itself, but still. He wasn't normally the kind of person to be put at ease with others right off the bat. Hell, even with Vanessa, the woman he'd planned to spend the rest of his life with, it had taken a while to warm up. And it had been months before he'd felt as comfortable with her as he had with Shelby in the first few minutes.

He made himself move toward her at the same time she began taking steps toward him. They met somewhere in the middle, near a display of nursing bras that would make most men turn away in awkward embarrassment, but which Cameron barely noticed after so many months working on Bedrock.

"How'd it go this morning?" he said. "Or should I ask?"

She expelled a restless sound. "It was…weird," she told him. "But I don't mind you asking. I thought I wanted to be alone to work through it all, but now, suddenly, I think maybe it would be good to talk about it."

"Are your half siblings at least okay people?"

She nodded. "They all seem nice, actually. Though one wasn't there and is supposed to come in tomorrow. I'm kind of surprised we all got along as well as we did. Our mothers, on the other hand…" Her eyes went wide. "Boy, talk about different personalities. I would have thought my father would have a type, you know? Most people seem to. But wow, he couldn't have found three more different women to marry and start a family with. God only knows what his mistress is going to be like once we find her."

"We?" Cameron said, confused. "Aren't the attorneys working on that?"

Shelby chuckled, but there wasn't much humor in the sound. "You'd think, wouldn't you? But therein lies a story that is very interesting."

Cameron grinned. "So you got lunch plans?"

Shelby smiled back. And this time, she did seem kind of happy. "Sounds like I'm about to make some."

"Just let me settle up with Flora for some things I'm getting to outfit the new Bedrock location we're opening up in Lubbock."

Hearing her name, the woman appeared behind the counter, looking cool and professional with her dark hair fastened at her nape in some kind of bun, her long-sleeved dress the color of espresso. She had a curious gleam in her dark eyes, though, as she looked at him and Shelby being so chummy.

Cameron paid for his purchases, made arrangements for their delivery, then he and Shelby ambled down Emerald Ridge Boulevard to Francesca's Bar and Grill. Once they were seated and had placed their orders for sandwiches and iced tea, Cameron settled in to hear about her morning. But her attention at the moment had been captured by a family at the next table, a young mother, father and a little boy who looked to Cameron's admittedly untrained eye to be around two. The child was trying to eat spaghetti and not doing a particularly tidy job of it while his parents laughed good-naturedly and tried to contain the mess. Shelby was smiling as she watched, a wistful, kind of faraway smile, as if she were looking at her not-too-distant future with little Spud.

And instead of mentioning anything specific about what had taken place at the meeting earlier that day, she said, "I never thought it would happen like this."

Confused, Cameron asked, "What? Your father's death? Finding out about your new extended family?"

Shelby turned to look at him now and shook her head. "No. About starting my own family. I never thought I'd be doing this all by myself. I guess I just always assumed I'd do things the traditional way, you know? Fall in love, get married, buy a house, *then* start a family and live happily ever after with my Prince Charming and our passel of little rug rats. Instead, I'm going to be a single mom trying to figure things out on my own."

Cameron sympathized. He'd kinda felt that way about his own life until everything with Vanessa went south. The two of them had talked about trying for a baby within the first few years of their marriage and had even looked at a few houses to purchase after they tied the knot that would be big enough for a family of at least four, maybe five.

"But you know what's really weird?" Shelby asked as she propped an elbow on the table to cradle her chin in her hand.

Frankly, there were a lot of weird things going on in

Shelby Fortune's life right now, so Cameron couldn't have answered that question if he tried. He only shook his head.

"What's strange is that, when I was a little girl, I used to love to dream about my wedding day."

"That's not weird at all," he said gently. "I think a lot of people dream about their wedding day when they're kids."

She nodded. "That's true. But that's not the weird part. It's that I had all of it down to the last detail. The dress, the veil, the music and flowers...being the center of attention." She laughed lightly. "Probably came from the same place in my personality that all the pageant stuff came from. But I did love thinking about it."

"There's nothing wrong with that," he reiterated.

"Maybe not," she acknowledged. "But even though I knew all those details and could picture it all so perfectly—that the dress would have a lace bodice and big tulle skirt, that I would walk down an aisle strewn with yellow rose petals and silver glitter to the Chicks' 'Cowboy Take Me Away,' that I would carry a bouquet of bluebonnets and coreopsis—I never once imagined who would be waiting for me at the altar." She sat up straight in her chair again, her gaze never leaving Cameron's. "That's weird, right? You'd think if I knew what kind of dress and music and flowers I wanted for the ceremony with absolute precision, I would have at least had *some* idea of the person I wanted to marry. I mean, I wanted a song about cowboys, for Pete's sake. But not once did I think about marrying one. Or anyone else."

Cameron thought about his own almost-wedding and realized he hadn't planned any of it. Vanessa had done all that. Which, yeah, wasn't all that weird, since she was the bride, and weddings tended to fall into the bride's purview, but in hindsight, he would have thought she would at least consult him on a few things. She'd just said one day that she'd reserved Rosewood Mansion at Turtle Creek for the ceremony on Christmas Day and the Ritz-Carlton Hotel for the reception afterward and told him what time to show up. He hadn't even known how many people he was allowed to invite until a week before she sent out save-the-date cards—and it had been significantly fewer than she was inviting herself.

Not that that last part mattered much. Cameron had barely known as many people as the total she gave him. But it had sort of occurred to him at that point just how little input he was being given into a day that was going to be, for him, as big a milestone as it was for her.

"I had no idea what kind of person I wanted to spend my whole life with," Shelby continued, thankfully scattering his thoughts. "I only thought about the act of getting married. And then the family and the house and the happily-ever-after. But now, I don't know if I'll have any of those things. Well, except for the family. Even if it only ever ends up being me and Spud, that's family, right?"

"It absolutely is," Cameron agreed.

For some reason, though, Shelby didn't look as if she believed that statement coming from either of them.

"I just hope I don't make too many mistakes," she said softly. "It would be so much easier if I wasn't doing this alone." Her eyes suddenly filled with tears, but she quickly swiped them away and forced a chuckle. "Listen to me. So maudlin. Must be the pregnancy hormones. Everything is fine. I'll be fine. It will all be..." She inhaled a shaky breath and let it out slowly. "Fine. I just need to figure out how I'm going to tell everyone and go from there. One step at a time, right?"

Cameron couldn't help wondering if the way Shelby felt right now was the way his birth mother must have had after realizing she would be a single mother with no help from anyone else, either. Yeah, Shelby's family and financial situation were infinitely better than Rue Evans's had been, but feeling scared and alone was feeling scared and alone, regardless of the exterior trappings.

He agreed with her, though, that she would be fine. Yes, she would make mistakes—everyone did, whether it was with parenting or something else—but she would learn and grow from them, and her relationship with Spud would be stronger for it. Even so, he wished there was something he could do to help.

Because that was what he did these days, he reminded himself. He helped pregnant women who were on their own and needed assistance. That was all there was to his motivation in wanting to help Shelby, too. Never mind that she wasn't nearly as underprivileged as the women Bedrock normally reached out to. She was a single mom. That was enough. His motivations had nothing to do with anything except that. They certainly had nothing to do with how lost and alone Shelby looked just then, even if she wasn't, technically, lost or alone.

Not sure what possessed him to do it, Cameron heard himself ask, "Do you want me to go with you when you tell your mother and sister about your pregnancy?"

He would have thought she would politely decline or even be a little put off by what she might see as an intrusion. Instead, she suddenly looked extremely relieved.

"Oh, Cameron, would you?" she asked. "That would be so kind of you. I would love to have you there with me."

He told himself it was a bad idea, in spite of being the one to suggest it. This was a family thing between Shelby and her mother and sister. And, eventually, her new extended family of half siblings, too. Cameron had no place in any of that. Nor would he ever. Thanks to his experience with Vanessa, it was going to be a long, long time before he trusted someone enough to share his life with her forever. Hell, he wasn't sure he'd ever be able to open himself up to anyone like that again.

But Shelby looked so happy after hearing his offer, there was no way he could rescind it now. And hell, why would he? He was Shelby's friend. He for sure liked and trusted her enough to be that. It wasn't like they were planning a life together here. He wasn't her baby's father or the man she wanted to spend her life with. He didn't have to go all in. Just be there for her for a little while.

"I'll be happy to," he told her. And, strangely, he realized he was. Happy. For the first time in a long time, he was enjoying spending time with a woman. He'd almost forgotten how good that could feel.

Shelby beamed. "Can we go after lunch?" she asked hopefully.

"Of course."

"Maybe it will cheer up Mama and Jillian. With all the stuff about my father, it would be nice for us to have something happy to focus on." She sighed with much contentment. "Thank you, Cameron. I owe you big for this."

"You don't owe me anything."

"I owe you more than you will ever know," she insisted. "You've done more for me in a few days than Spud's father did in the year I was with him. Just know that I appreciate it."

Cameron dipped his head forward in both acceptance of and gratitude for her compliment. She was being extravagant with her praise. He wasn't doing any more for her than he would do for any of the mothers who came through the Bedrock program. Funny, though, how even though all of those women came from disadvantaged backgrounds and Shelby came from one of privilege, she seemed to need him more than any of the others did.

Because she's your friend, a voice inside him reminded him. But suddenly, she felt like a whole lot more than that.

As Shelby preceded Cameron through the back door of the Fortune home and into the kitchen, she was still wondering why she had invited him along for what was going to be a huge family reveal. She'd known from his surprise at her acceptance of his offer that he'd only made it out of politeness and had expected her to decline. But she hadn't realized how nervous she was about telling her mother and Jillian until he told her he'd come along. The idea of having a hand to hold—figuratively, of course—had just made her feel better somehow. And she still couldn't shake the notion of how close she felt to Cameron after such a short time. But there it was all the same. Some people, she supposed, just had that gift of making others feel good the minute they made contact. That was Cameron Waite.

Who looked incredibly handsome today, she thought, not for the first time. His blond hair was irresistibly tousled from him removing his Stetson when they came in, and her fingers itched to run through the silky tresses to tame them. But his own hand got there first, smoothing them out as he set his hat on the kitchen island. Today he wore dark wash jeans that hugged his lean hips and thighs like a lover's caress, and a pale blue Western shirt—a few shades lighter than the startling cerulean of his eyes—unbuttoned at the neck, giving her just a peek of what lay beneath. Once again, her hands wanted to betray her, tucking themselves beneath the collar of that shirt to unfasten it button by button, cupping lovingly over his nape as she pulled him close for another kiss. Only this time, she wouldn't stop kissing him. This time she would taste him to the depths of his soul, explore every inch of him she could reach, then take him by the hand and lead him up to her bedroom where she would—

"Your house is amazing," he said, disrupting her thoughts.

For which, *of course*, she was grateful. Tasting and touching Cameron was the last thing she should be thinking about doing. Pregnancy hormones really could be ferocious sometimes. Ahem.

"You've only seen it from the outside and the kitchen," she reminded him. "I should give you the grand tour. The living room, the dining room, the library, my bed…ah, I mean…the sunroom. Daddy and Mama went all out with the place after he bought it."

"I had no idea mansions like this existed in Emerald Ridge."

"Fortune and Daughters Ranch has the only one," she said. "It was here before the town even was. You can see a bit more of it on the way upstairs. There's a room up there Jillian and I always called 'Mama's room' because she's the only one who ever used it, and it's always been kind of a retreat for her. Books, music, big-screen TV. I know they were planning a rom-com marathon to take their minds off the meeting this morning."

Cameron nodded. "Sounds like a good way to escape your troubles for a bit."

"The whole room is an escape," she said as they made their way toward the stairs. "I spent more than one day up there when I was a kid, crying my eyes out over something while Mama comforted me. She and I shared a lot of ice cream over things like Cooper Tucker asking Lanelle Hilliard instead of me to the sixth-grade spring dance or when Emmy Crawford won Safe Boating Queen, and I came in second."

"Oof," Cameron said. "Tough times."

Shelby chuckled. "Yeah, sometimes I don't know how I survived." She looked thoughtful. "It all seems so silly now, even though, at the time, it was the end-all and be-all of, oh, everything. I know Spud will have his little age-appropriate turmoil while he's growing up, but I hope I can help guide him through it all so that he doesn't come out of it thinking things like, oh… his *image*, for instance is more important than his character. And doing the right thing is hard sometimes, but will always put you in a better place. And I hope he'll always know that the people who love him will love him forever, unconditionally."

"I think with a mom like you, Shelby, that's gonna be a given."

They made their way up to the second floor and down a hallway past hers and Jillian's bedrooms and their father's home office, until they reached the room at the very end. It was cozy and smaller than most of the house's expansive rooms, painted sage green with a toile sofa and chairs and a creamy rug spanning the dark wood floor. A painting of a bowl of roses hung above the sofa, surrounded by smaller images of other showy flowers. The accents were all super feminine, from the brass lamps to the tasseled throw pillows to the fringed curtains on the opposite side. The room was lush and old-fashioned, but also comfy and warm. Just walking into it again made Shelby feel calmer.

Her sister and mother were on the sofa, and the closing credits of what Shelby knew was *The Princess Diaries*—she'd heard that piano piece a million times—scrolled by on the screen of the TV tucked into one corner. Looked like they had forgone the pomegranate tea for a bottle of wine instead, as each had a glass of something ruby red sitting on the table in front of them, along with an open bottle from the local winery, Leonetti Vineyards. Not that Shelby blamed them. Had she not been pregnant, she would have marched back down to the kitchen for another bottle and two more glasses for her and Cameron to join them.

They looked up when Shelby entered, smiling at her appearance until Cameron walked in behind her, whereupon they looked confused.

"Mama, Jillian," she said, "um, I'd like y'all to meet my, ah, my…" She suddenly realized she had no idea how to introduce him.

"I'm Shelby's friend, Cameron," he said when he must have noticed her distress. "Cameron Waite." He lifted a hand in a quick hello, then dropped it back to his side.

"Right," Shelby agreed. "This is my *friend*. My friend Cameron." She turned to look at him, and he gave her a reassuring smile. "Cameron," she continued, turning back to the others, "this is my mother, Agatha Fortune, and my sister, Jillian Fortune."

"Mrs. Fortune," he greeted Agatha with a deferential dip of his head. "Ms. Fortune," he added, doing the same for Jillian. "I'm so sorry about your all's loss. I never met Mr. Fortune, but from what Shelby's told me about him, he sounds like he was quite the impressive individual."

Agatha beamed at the compliment he paid Archibald, but Jillian only threw Shelby a knowing look.

"That's one way to put it," her sister said. "And please. It's Jillian. None of this 'Ms.' stuff. It's nice to meet you, Cameron."

Her mother echoed the sentiment, but both women wore curious expressions, as if they couldn't understand why Shelby was bringing a *friend* home, especially on a day like today.

"Would you like a glass of wine, dear?" her mother asked Shelby. "It's been a week, after all."

"No, thanks, Mama," she said.

"Mr. Waite?" her mother asked.

"I'm good, ma'am, thank you. But please, call me Cameron."

Jillian and her mother were still looking at Shelby expectantly, so she told them, "I ran into Cameron while I was window-shopping in Emerald Ridge, and since you two took the car after the meeting with the Inlands this morning, he was kind enough to offer me a ride home."

Which, she thought, was actually a perfectly good reason why he could be here. It just wasn't the right reason.

So she continued, "But the real reason he's here is to help me give y'all some news."

Now her mother and sister looked at her even more curiously. *Just say it, Shelby*, she told herself. It was good news after all. Maybe it was going to take a minute for them to realize that, but when they did, it was going to be a bright spot in what had been a very dark couple of days.

When Shelby still didn't say anything, though, her mother asked, "And what news is that, dear?"

"I'm, um..." She looked at Cameron, who gave her an encouraging nod, then back at her mother and sister. "I'm, ah... I'm kind of..." *Just say it, for Pete's sake!* "I'm pregnant."

For a moment, neither her mother nor sister reacted at all. They just continued to stare at her, as if she hadn't spoken. Then they looked surprised, then kind of shocked. Finally, they shared a glance before turning their attention back to Shelby, both looking as if they must have misheard.

As if to punctuate that, Jillian said, "I'm sorry, you're *what*?"

"I'm gonna have a baby," she told them. "A boy. In June. Mama, you're gonna be a grandmama. And, Jillian, you're gonna be an auntie."

There was another minute of stunned silence, then both Jillian and her mother looked at Cameron. And the look that came over their faces then was—

Oh, no. They thought Cameron was the father! That the reason she'd brought him home to introduce him was because it was him, not Dylan, who had—

"No, I'm not having Cameron's baby!" she fairly shouted. "I'm having Dylan's baby! Cameron is just here for moral support! Because he's my...um, my...uh..."

"Her friend," Cameron said again. His voice was laced with both relief and humor, though, as if he'd realized at the same time Shelby did what her mother and sister were concluding about him and was happy to have the record put straight.

But her reassurance didn't seem to reassure anyone else. Her sister and mother looked even more confused by that.

"Oh, crap," Shelby said with much understatement.

Cameron reached for her hand and laced their fingers together, as if realizing she needed a bit more support. Jillian, she noticed, clocked the gesture. Big-time. Another long silence followed—then Jillian and Agatha looked at each other. Then at Shelby, and back at each other. And then, at the same moment, they broke out into huge smiles and jumped up from the sofa.

"You're going to have a baby?" her mother cried in clear delight. "I'm going to be a grandmother?"

She crossed the room to wrap both arms around Shelby and hugged her so tight, Shelby had to let go of Cameron to wrap her arms around Agatha instead. Though, she couldn't help noticing, not before he gave her fingers another affectionate squeeze. Her mother must have felt the baby bump when she embraced her, because she drew far enough away to look down at Shelby's abdomen. Then her grin widened, and she cupped her hand over the soft swell of her belly.

"Oh, my goodness," she said softly, her voice filled with awe. "You *are* pregnant. How could I not have noticed?"

Jillian joined them, roping an arm around her sister's waist to pull her close. Her hand joined their mother's on her abdomen, and she shook her head in clear astonishment.

"How could *I* not have noticed?" she said. "I always notice stuff like this."

Shelby's hand joined theirs, so that all three of them were cradling the new life growing inside her. "Well, once I started showing," she said, "I deliberately started picking out loose stuff from the closet. I didn't want anyone to suspect until I could make it public."

"I can't believe you're as far along as you are," Jillian said. "Why didn't you tell us? Have you even told Dylan?" Her sister sobered the minute the question was out of her mouth. "This is why you two split up, isn't it? He left because he can't be a grown-up."

Shelby nodded. "'Fraid so."

"What?" her mother said, clearly aghast. "He just up and left when he found out he was going to be a father?"

Shelby felt a hand open lightly at the small of her back, as if giving her more support, and she knew immediately it was Cameron's. When she turned to look at him, his expression had changed from happy good humor to something almost angry. As if he wished he could step outside with Dylan and give the guy a piece of his mind for bailing so completely on his own child. Or maybe what Cameron wanted to give him was a piece of his fist. Hard to say for sure.

She looked back at her mother. "He's known for months, Mama. He found out I was pregnant the day I did. I mean, we were both surprised, but where I came around to really loving the idea, he..." She shrugged. "He didn't. It just took him until last week to admit that he doesn't want to be a father, and he took off for Austin."

The hand on Shelby's back splayed wider, sending a spiral of warmth winding through her.

"Well, that's too damned bad," Jillian said. "He's going to be a father. He needs to step up."

Now Shelby shook her head. "No, it's fine. Things between us had been kind of rocky for a couple months when it happened. Looking back, I realize he and I wouldn't have made it, with or without my getting pregnant. And I'd rather he be out of the picture than to be a reluctant father to our…to *my*…child. Kids aren't stupid. Little Spud would have picked up immediately on Dylan's resentment and realized his father didn't want him around."

In spite of the melancholy sentiment in the statement, Jillian's lips twitched. "Spud? Please tell me you're not going to be naming my little nephew Spud."

Shelby heard Cameron's chuckle—it chorused with hers—and turned to look at him again. Now he was smiling. But he hadn't moved his hand from her back. And she was really happy about that.

"Of course I'm not naming him Spud," Shelby assured her sister. She looked at Jillian again. "At least not once I decide on a name. But Dr. Chavez said after my sonogram the other day that he's about the size of a baked potato right now, so Spud just kind of fit."

Her mother laughed at that. "You know, Shelby, you were 'Peanut' for the longest time after I had my first ultrasound with you. And you," she said as she turned to Jillian, "were 'Dumpling.' So don't be judging your sister's choice."

"I'm not," Jillian denied. "It's just that nicknames have a habit of hanging around. I'm not sure I want to be introducing my nephew as Spud all the time. Especially after he becomes the CEO of a Fortune 500 company. Or a neurosurgeon. Or President of these here United States."

"I told her the same thing," Cameron said. "He's gonna wind up being cited in scientific journals someday as 'astrophysicist and solver of the mystery of dark matter, Spud Fortune.'"

"No," Shelby said, laughing, "I already told you he's going to bring about world peace."

"If anyone can do it," Jillian said, "it'll be one of the Texas Fortunes."

"I still can't believe Dylan left," Agatha grumbled. "That he would turn his back on his own baby. On *you*," she told Shelby.

She lifted one shoulder and let it drop. "Like I said, he was already showing signs of not being a good guy. Maybe that's just how most men are. How life is," she said, trying to be philosophical. "I mean, look at what happened with Daddy. Maybe true love doesn't exist, and we should all stop thinking it does."

"I hear that," Jillian said, her tone only half joking.

"No," Agatha told her daughters adamantly. "We can't let your father's betrayal and lies—or Dylan's horrible behavior, for that matter—dictate how we all feel about life and love. This baby is a fresh start for our family." After a moment, she added, "And so are your new half siblings, as strange as that seems. Hearing about your father's…*escapades*…has been difficult, but his behavior doesn't reflect on anything, or anybody, but himself. You must both always keep your hearts open to the possibility of love."

Don't look at Cameron, don't look at Cameron, do not *look at Cameron.* The admonition hurtled through Shelby's brain like a locomotive, even though she knew love was the last thing either of them was feeling for each other. But she couldn't help herself. She immediately looked at Cameron. Who was gazing back at her. In a way she couldn't for the life of her fathom.

He only smiled, though—a little sadly, she couldn't help thinking—and said, "Your mother is right. You can't let other people's ugly behavior taint your beliefs about yourself or anything else."

You can't let others, Shelby echoed to herself. *Your* beliefs. *Your*self. The way he spoke, Cameron sounded like what he'd really meant to say was *we* can't let others and *our* beliefs and *our*selves. As if he were speaking from experience. She wondered whose ugly behavior had tainted his own beliefs. And she wondered if he still felt that way, in spite of his insistence to the contrary.

When she glanced at Jillian, she expected to see her sister reacting with her usual wry dismissal of matters of the heart. Jillian had never really seemed to take any of that seriously. She'd dated plenty, usually the trust fund guys their social circle brought them into contact with—guys who weren't exactly purpose-driven or deep thinkers. Certainly nothing with any of those men had ever turned into some big, epic romance. And with the few semi-serious relationships Shelby had enjoyed herself, Jillian had always kind of seemed to pooh-pooh the whole idea of happily ever after.

Instead of looking wry, though, her sister looked as if she were a million miles away. As if she were thinking about something—someone?—that her mother's words had stirred in her brain. Maybe there was a new guy in her life that Shelby didn't know about? Or maybe Shelby was wrong, and Jillian really had cared about someone in the past who hurt her? She and her sister had been close when they were young. They were still close. But they'd both gone their own ways over the last few years and had both had other commitments and interests.

Really, when was the last time the two of them sat down to talk about stuff the way sisters were supposed to? Once everything with the new Fortunes in town settled down, Shelby was going to invite Jillian to lunch or dinner, just the two of them, so that they could reconnect.

"A baby," her mother said again, beaming in her delight. "A grandbaby. Baby Spud." She smiled again. "Oh, Shelby, I'm so happy for you. For all of us. This has made a terrible week so much better."

Jillian snapped out of her funk at the comment and smiled, too. "It really has, Shelby. If there's anything you need..."

For some reason, that comment made Shelby look at Cameron again. And he looked right back at her. Or maybe he'd never stopped looking at her. She couldn't say for sure.

"I'll let you know," she said in response to her sister's statement. Funny, though, how she was still looking at Cameron when she did.

Chapter Eight

The decor for Captain's restaurant was as elegant as the rest of Emerald Ridge Hotel, Shelby noted as she and Jillian strode through its marble foyer three nights after meeting their new half siblings for the first time. White linen tablecloths cloaked every table in the restaurant and walnut-backed chairs were tufted with pearly cushions. Walnut, too, were the paneled walls on two sides, dotted with half-moon wall sconces under elegant track lighting in the ceiling. Another wall was actually floor-to-ceiling windows, offering a breathtaking view of Emerald Ridge beyond. Tonight, it looked as if someone had scattered diamonds across it, lit up as it was in the winter darkness.

Shelby and Jillian had eaten here many times, both as individuals with friends or dates, or as sisters with their parents. So they were greeted warmly when they reached the host stand by Javier, the dark-haired, dark-suited maître d' who was standing behind it. Of course, Javier also knew them both from elementary school, though he had been three grades behind Shelby, so that helped.

"Miss Shelby and Miss Jillian," he greeted them in spite of their shared childhood history. "How nice to see you both again."

"Hi, Javier," Shelby said. "And will you please drop

the 'Miss' stuff? I remember tying your shoelaces for you on the playground when we were kids."

He grinned at that, one that momentarily abandoned the formal maître d' mien. "Sorry, girlfriends, but I have a job description I gotta follow. Bosses are here tonight." He straightened to his previous posture, tidying the Windsor knot at his throat that in no way needed tidying. "I believe, Miss Shelby, that you have a reservation this evening, yes? For five?"

Shelby rolled her eyes. "Fine. Yes, I do. Thank you, Javier."

"Excellent. Two of your party have already arrived. I'll show you both to your table."

"Thanks, dude," Jillian told him with a smile of her own as he preceded them into the restaurant proper.

The sisters had turned out in appropriate attire for the occasion, even though Captain's didn't have a dress code, because they both liked dressing up for things like this. Jillian wore loose tailored black trousers and a silky emerald blouse that brought out the green in her hazel eyes tonight. Shelby, now that her pregnancy was no longer a secret, had opted for a clingy red velvet wrap dress that put her baby bump firmly in the spotlight, literally front and center. She really was going to have to start rethinking the heels, though, she decided as they made their approach to a round table in the corner where Hayes and Madeline were seated. Her center of gravity was shifting by the minute.

Their half siblings had dressed for the night, too, Hayes in a chocolate brown Western-style suit and bolo tie and Madeline in an amethyst jacquard dress. They were speaking quietly at the table when the sisters arrived, the open menus on the table before them currently being ignored. As Shelby drew closer, she was surprised to find that the two of them weren't discussing their father's death or the terms of his will or even Lianna Dunhill, but were instead remarking on how much they had been enjoying discovering Emerald Ridge during the few days they'd been in town.

"And the Coffee Connection," Madeline was saying. "Did you try their churros? There's something mixed in with the sugar and cinnamon I can't put my finger on, but it makes such a difference."

"Cardamom," Shelby said as Javier pulled out the chair beside Madeline so that Jillian could sit down. "They mix in a little cardamom."

"That's it!" Madeline said triumphantly. "Now that you say that, I can totally taste it."

"Shelby and I have their recipe if you want it," Jillian told the other woman as she folded herself into the chair. "Our cook, Mrs. Pulaski, sweet-talked them out of it."

"Email me that, will you?" Madeline asked. "I know it will be super popular with all the caterers I work with."

"Happy to," Jillian told her.

It was only the second time the half siblings had met face-to-face, and Shelby couldn't help thinking how weird it was that they were all talking right now as if they'd grown up together. Javier moved to the chair beside Jillian and pulled it out, too, for Shelby to sit. Before she did, she noticed Madeline's gaze go from Jillian's face to her own, then drop down to Shelby's torso.

"Wait," Madeline said, her curious gaze moving to Shelby's face again. "Are you…?"

She didn't finish the question, though whether that

was because she was afraid it would be invasive or misconstrued, Shelby wasn't sure. Even so, she knew what the other woman wanted to ask.

"Yes," she told her half sister with a smile as she folded herself into her chair and let Javier scoot her in. "I'm pregnant. Four months along. Due in June."

Javier bent forward long enough to whisper his congratulations, then smiled at the table and made a discreet maître d' exit. Shelby could tell Madeline wanted to ask more, but she only echoed Javier's congratulations. Though the word from her had just the tiniest inquisitive inflection, as if she wasn't sure she should make it a statement or a question. Fair enough, Shelby thought. They all might be talking like family at the moment, but they were still pretty much strangers. There was no way Madeline could know the circumstances of Shelby's situation and whether or not the pregnancy had been planned or was welcomed.

Hayes, however, seemed to have no qualms at all about inquiring further. "I didn't realize you were married, Shelby," he said. "There was nothing about that in the dossier Mr. Inland gave us."

Shelby could tell by the way he winced that their half sister on his other side had just kicked him under the table.

Shelby chuckled, surprised that she didn't feel embarrassed or ashamed by the question. In fact, she was unbelievably happy to be in the state she was in. It hadn't been that long ago that she'd thought she would be mortified by the public at large knowing the circumstances of her condition and worried that she would have to hide her face wherever she went as an abandoned, unwed mother. Oh, dearie dear. And although she was sure there had been, and continued to be, some less-than-flattering talk about her, um, indiscretion and Dylan's desertion, it was mostly going on between people who didn't have anything better to do with their time than gossip. Also, she just plain didn't care. The people who mattered most, the ones Shelby loved who loved her back, had been nothing but delighted and supportive.

"That's because I'm not married," she told her half siblings matter-of-factly. "In fact, my baby's father hightailed it out of town a couple weeks ago, and we are both better off for it."

"Yeah, he was a jerk," Jillian said.

This was news to Shelby. "I thought you liked Dylan."

Her sister shook her head as she perused the choices on her menu. "Only because you did. You really are better off without him." Now she looked up and smiled sweetly. "Especially since you have that nice Cameron Waite. Now him I *do* like."

Shelby did, too. Probably more than she should. She still wasn't sleeping well at night thanks to *aaalll* the times she'd replayed in her mind the single kiss they'd shared. And how perfect his mouth had felt against her own. And the way his hand had been so warm and comforting on her back when she broke the news of her pregnancy to her family.

And then there were the other thoughts that had not only kept her awake, but had permeated her dreams, too, once she finally did fall asleep. Thoughts about his sea-glass blue eyes and tousled blond hair, his broad shoulders and the salient muscles of his forearms. And how, in her dreams, she unbuttoned his shirt to reveal more of those muscles so she could trace her fingertips over each elegant one. Then move lower, to the waistband of his jeans and flip open the snap, then draw down the zipper slowly, slowly, oh…so slowly, until she could tuck her hand inside and—

Um, where was she? Right. About to sit down to dinner with her family, so she should definitely stop remembering her late-night thoughts of Cameron and his many, *many* delectable attributes. And why was the restaurant so hot all of a sudden? She should mention that to Javier on their way out, how there seemed to be a problem with the air conditioning.

Anyway.

"I do not have Cameron Waite," Shelby told her sister. Even if she, you know, kind of wished she did have him. In more ways than one. Ahem.

Jillian's smile went absolutely saccharine. "Oh, don't you?"

Shelby was about to object again, but their server, a young woman dressed in the usual restaurant livery of crisp white shirt, black trousers and bow tie, approached and asked if they would like a drink before dinner. Jillian ordered a glass of Pinot Noir while Shelby asked for sparkling water.

After she left, Hayes asked the table at large, "Has anybody discovered anything new—or anything at all—about Lianna Dunhill since the last time we saw each other?"

Shelby glanced at the empty chair between her and Hayes. "Aren't we going to wait until your brother gets here to talk about that?"

Hayes looked a little uncomfortable. "Yeah, about that. Penn isn't going to be joining us tonight. He's not in Emerald Ridge yet."

The three women exchanged alarmed looks.

"When is he coming?" Jillian asked.

Hayes blew out an exasperated breath. "I'll be honest. He may not be joining us at all."

"But he has to," Shelby said, alarmed.

Madeline nodded. "Otherwise, none of us will collect our inheritance, and our mothers could end up on the streets."

"I explained all that to him," Hayes said. "But he's pretty shook up. He *really* doesn't want to have anything to do with it."

"Well, tell him it's not up to him," Shelby said. "Change his mind."

"I'm trying," he told them. "So is Mom. Maybe between the two of us, we can get him to see sense."

"You have to," Madeline said. "Otherwise, we'll lose everything."

"I just need a little more time," Hayes said. "For now, the four of us can start comparing notes about Lianna Dunhill…"

Shelby and Jillian exchanged a wary glance. If Penn Fortune didn't join the rest of them, he could ruin it for everyone concerned—Archibald's children *and* his wives. All three Mrs. Fortunes had devoted their lives to their families, never earning a living. Agatha's entire source of income had always been an allowance their father deposited monthly into her personal account. Their house wasn't even in her name—only their father's. If her allowance came to a halt, she would have nothing to sustain her and be left without a roof over her head.

Certainly Shelby and Jillian could and would take care of her if it came to that, but Agatha Fortune was the kind of woman who would consider herself a burden to her children under such circumstances. And that was the last thing she wanted to be.

"I couldn't find out a thing about Lianna," Madeline said, pulling Shelby back to the matter at hand. "She lived here in Emerald Ridge when the internet wasn't nearly the monster it is now, and she was a poor waitress who probably couldn't even afford a computer. There's no mention of her online anywhere. She certainly has no digital footprint that I could find. It's like she never existed."

"Shelby and I ran into the same problem," Jillian said. "I mean, neither of us has really had a lot of time to put into it yet, but we did do some digging and found nothing."

"Jillian's right," Shelby said. "I even contacted a friend of mine who works for Vital Statistics to see if she could find out anything, but there's nothing for any Lianna Dunhill in the whole state of Texas. Not even a birth certificate or a marriage license. So she wasn't born here. At least not with that name. And if she got married, which she may have, then that didn't happen here, either."

"She may have changed her name another way," Hayes suggested.

"Not in Texas, she didn't," Shelby told him. "There would be a record of that, too."

"Maybe she didn't change it legally," Madeline said. "And if that's the case, there won't be a mention of her out there anywhere."

Hayes thought for a minute. "You know, there's a lot of stuff online you can't get to because it's behind a paywall or you have to be a member of some kind. And probably a lot of sites none of us would even think to look at. Maybe what we should do is hire a private investigator."

"I still don't understand why the Inlands haven't already done that," Madeline said.

"Because they know Daddy wanted *us* to be the ones to find our half sibling," Shelby told her.

Jillian nodded. "Dad obviously wanted all of us to find out about each other and get to know each other after his death—at which point he wouldn't be around to suffer any consequences—and this is his way of making sure we have no choice but to do that."

Shelby agreed. She'd become convinced of that even without asking Mr. Inland to confirm it.

"Why would he do that?" Madeline asked. "He had to know it would cause a lot of anger and hurt feelings for the truth to come out. Why didn't he just let the attorneys take care of everything, divvy up his estate between all his widows and children without telling any of us the truth, and then let us all go our merry way none the wiser?"

Jillian shook her head. "Why did he do any of the things he did?" she countered. "None of it makes any sense. I mean, to marry three women, all within a year of each other? To start families with them, knowing only Shelby and I would be his legal offspring and our mother his only lawful widow? What makes someone do something like that?"

"Someone who craved a lot of love," Shelby said before she could stop herself. "Someone who was terrified of ending up alone."

It was only in that moment that she realized how true that must have been for their father. It was no secret in Emerald Ridge that Archibald Fortune had grown up dirt-poor with parents who hadn't been the most stable people in the world and that he'd lost them when he was only fourteen. He'd had to find work in one place or another while he was still pretty much a child himself. It was only through a little luck and a lot of determination and hard work that he made his first million when he was only twenty-five.

Yes, their father had clawed his way to the top and made a pile of money, but he hadn't been quite so fortunate when it came to finding people to love him. Growing up, his family had been emotionally detached, and the town he called home had overlooked him. After being granted a small sum of money from a relative who was more of a stranger, she'd told him not to expect anything more. Everything Archibald had achieved, he'd managed it alone.

He must have met all three of his wives at about the same time, if he'd married them all in such a short time frame, one after another. Maybe he'd feared he wouldn't be able to hang on to all of them, so he'd collected as many as he could, just in case. Then he'd taken a mistress along the way, too, another woman whose affection and company he had obviously craved. Maybe he'd feared the families he started with those women would leave him alone the same way the family he'd had as a boy would, so he'd tried to make as many of those as he could, as well.

It was actually kind of sad, now that Shelby thought about it. She'd been thinking her father was arrogant and selfish and entitled, behaving the way he had, starting three different families. But maybe what it all came down to was that, deep down inside, he was just a scared, lonely little boy afraid of losing everything—of losing everyone.

Jillian, Madeline and Hayes all seemed to give her statement some thought, though none of them said anything more to agree or disagree. Then their server returned with Jillian's glass of wine and Shelby's water, and the moment was gone, replaced by an industrious air of let's-get-down-to-brass-tacks.

"I know a good PI in Houston," Hayes said. "He's done some excellent work for me vetting people I have working for me. When you work with children, like my organization does, you have to be extremely careful who you hire. This guy can find the dirtiest dirt on anyone. He might be able to scare up a thing or two about Lianna Dunhill."

"I have great Google-fu when I put my mind to it and have the time," Shelby added. "I can dig up *a lot* of info on the 'net, given enough time to do it. Kinda have to be able to do that when you're in the pageant circuit, to size up the competition. I can do some deeper dives online in a few places to see if Lianna *has* ever had any kind of online presence."

"And I can go old-school and hit the library and hall of records," Jillian offered. "I was a library aide at boarding school and in college." She grinned again. "I even know how to work a microfiche machine."

"I can look into that tract of land Dad owns that he wants to leave to Lianna's offspring," Madeline chimed in. "See if there actually *has* been anything filed about plans for its development or sale or anything else. Maybe I can at least find out more about its provenance."

The three women looked at Hayes.

"And Penn?" Shelby asked pointedly. "How can he contribute?"

Jillian nodded. "Since it goes without saying that your brother *will* be here to help, right?"

"If nothing else," Madeline added, "he can be the one who stays on top of everything we find and keeps it organized and files the reports with the Inlands."

Hayes nodded in deference to the women who outnumbered him. "I'll talk to him again."

"And you'll get him on board," Jillian said.

"And I'll get him on board," Hayes promised with a heavy sigh. "But I'll warn y'all... He's pretty damned weirded out about this whole thing. I'm still not sure he's come to terms yet with the bombshell Dad dropped on all of us."

"It has been pretty weird," Jillian agreed. "I mean, one day you're going about your life the way you have for decades, and the next, you realize your life is never going to be the same again."

"And in my case," Madeline said, "I've always thought I was an only child, and now suddenly I have four, maybe five siblings I never knew existed."

Hayes shook his head. "I can't imagine that. I mean, yeah, it's pretty dang odd having a bunch of sisters suddenly, but at least Penn and I have never been the only child. I guess it would be strange to wake up one morning and realize you're not alone in the world, after all."

"Hopefully, it's a nice realization, though, Madeline," Jillian said softly.

Their half sister smiled. "Now that the shock is wearing off, yeah. It is kinda nice. I always wanted a brother or sister when I was little, and now I have two of each."

Shelby thought about Cameron, about how he'd discovered his long-lost twin months ago but was still coming to terms with having a brother. Then again, for him, discovering an additional sibling had turned out to be one of the best things that ever happened to him. Maybe, at some point, all the newly united Fortunes would feel that way about themselves, too.

"Okay, then," she said to everyone at the table. "Looks like we have a plan in place, and we all know what to do. Now let's enjoy a nice dinner. Tomorrow, we'll get to work finding Lianna Dunhill. Tonight, though, let's just—" She honestly almost said *Let's just be a family*. But it was probably still a little early for that. So she only finished, "Tonight, let's just get to know each other better."

Chapter Nine

In spite of having practically moved to Emerald Ridge over the last couple of months, Cameron hadn't seen his brother, Drake, even in passing, for a couple of weeks when he ran into him on his way to Rusty's Hardware. As he rounded the corner onto the busy thoroughfare, whom should he see coming out of the very store he had planned to enter but his brother.

When Drake saw him, his face split into a wide grin, and the two men exchanged greetings and a good, solid, slap-on-the-back hug. Then Drake mentioned how he was on his way to Donatello's Pizzeria to grab a couple slices and a beer, and did Cameron want to join him? Since his errand had already been postponed once, he didn't see any reason why it couldn't be again, and the two men made their way down the block past a few more storefronts, to enter the restaurant that always seemed to be bustling.

"Long time, no see," Cameron said as he and his brother scooted into a booth, each automatically grabbing a menu from the half dozen tucked in between the condiments at one end.

"Speak for yourself," Drake told him. "I've seen you out and about in town a couple of times this week, always with a very attractive blonde."

At this, Cameron looked up curiously. "Why didn't you say anything?"

"I waved at you one time and actually called out a hello the second, but you walked right past me *both* times." Drake threw him a comically chastising look. "Something about having a very attractive blonde at your side, I'm guessing."

His brother had to be exaggerating. No way would he have not noticed if Drake said hello. Then he remembered just how captivating Shelby could be, and how very focused he'd been on her every time they ran into each other. Okay, *maybe* he could see not noticing a greeting from his brother on those occasions.

"So who *is* this attractive blonde?" his brother asked when Cameron didn't offer any enlightenment.

"Shelby Fortune," Cameron told him.

Now Drake looked even more surprised. Then he laughed. "Figures it would be a Fortune. This town is crawling with them."

"Present company included," Cameron couldn't help adding.

"Guess I haven't met her branch of the family yet," his brother said. "So she's our distant cousin or something?"

"*Your* distant cousin," Cameron corrected him. "I'm not a Fortune."

"Well, if she's my cousin, then she's kind of yours, too, by default."

"As long as it's not by DNA."

Now why would he have said that? What difference did it make if he and Shelby shared the same family tree? It wasn't like the two of them were planning on being any more to each other than friends.

Drake laughed again. "Yeah, that could turn into one of those over-the-top scandal documentaries pretty quick."

"Shelby and I are just friends," Cameron assured him. "And that's what we're going to stay."

Drake smiled. "Didn't look like that to me when I saw you. Though you did look pretty friendly."

"We're friends," Cameron repeated. "Neither of us is interested in starting anything with anyone. She's just coming off the kind of situation with her ex that I had with Vanessa not too long ago."

His brother only muttered a noncommittal sound at that, then turned his attention to the menu. "Damn, I can never decide what to order here. They have like twenty different pizzas."

Cameron looked at the selections, too. His brother was right. They had a little bit of everything. Finally, both men closed their menus at the same time, looked up and said, in chorus, "*La Festa della Carne*." Which, according to the menu, was Italian for *The Meat Fest*. In other words, all the meats they had that would fit on a pizza pie.

The brothers laughed. It wasn't the first time they'd been on the same wavelength about something. In fact, it was kind of scary still how similar the two men were after being raised hundreds of miles away from each other.

Their server came and went after they placed their orders—turned out they liked the same brand of beer, too—then they talked a bit about what they'd been up to since they last saw each other. Cameron filled in Drake on all the progress he was making with Bedrock, and Drake showed him all the latest photos of the baby he and his wife, Annelise, had recently welcomed into the world. It struck Cameron as he looked at them that this was what was in store for Shelby in the not-too-distant future. Soon, she'd be whipping out her phone to show him pics of little Spud every time he ran into her in town.

Then again, he might not be in town very often after her baby's arrival. He might be leaving Emerald Ridge—for good—before Spud even made an appearance. He really did need to get Bedrock up and running so he could go back to his job—to his life—in Dallas. Sure, he'd be back here to visit Drake and his family from time to time, and he and Shelby could make plans to visit on those occasions. But considering how much her world was going to change after her baby's arrival, and how little time she was going to have for anything besides her son, it might be tough for the two of them to do much more than wave hello as they passed on the street.

"So this Shelby Fortune," Drake said after their server returned with their beers, "how did the two of you meet?"

Cameron only meant to tell his brother about that morning outside Dr. Chavez's office when Shelby literally fell into his arms, but by the time he finished, he realized he'd told Drake nearly everything else, too. About the death of her father coming on the heels of their meeting. About her discovery of Archibald's other two families right on the heels of that. And finally, about how now she and her newly discovered half siblings were supposed to find what sounded like yet another half sibling who could be anywhere in the world...or might not exist at all.

Drake listened in stunned silence with every new addition to the story, then shook his head at its conclusion. "Wow," he said. "This is some week Shelby Fortune is having."

"And through it all, she's been surprisingly upbeat and

philosophical. I mean, yeah, there have been a couple of moments when it's almost gotten the better of her, but…"

He remembered again that unforgettable kiss the two of them shared in his penthouse earlier in the week. And how exhausted she'd looked, scrunched up by his front door when he arrived. But he also thought about how brave she'd been when she told her mother and sister about her pregnancy. And about how determined she was to make the best of her father's last wishes and work with Archibald Fortune's other families, even though a lot of people would be too filled with grief or resentment to manage it.

"But what?" Drake asked.

Only then did Cameron realize he never finished what he'd intended to say. Then again, he wasn't sure what he'd intended to say. He'd been too busy thinking about Shelby—how much her life had changed this week, and the even bigger shift that would come once she had her baby. And he found himself wishing he could shoulder some of the load for her. Take care of her, since she was going to have to be so focused on caring for others. Not just Spud, but her mother and sister, too, as they dealt with the loss of Archibald. And the other families she was suddenly tied to. Shelby was the kind of person who took the initiative and felt like she needed to be the one who was there for other people. He didn't think it would ever occur to her to be sure to take care of herself, too.

"I just wish I could help her out," he told his brother. "I mean, she's pretty amazing, but she's also got a lot on her plate right now."

"Then help her out," Drake said.

"Okay, number one, when?" Cameron asked. "I probably won't even be here in Emerald Ridge that much longer. I've been away from Dallas and Waite Financial for too long as it is. And number two, Shelby is adamant she can take care of herself. I don't think she'd accept help from anyone else."

Drake grinned. "Wow, sounds a lot like somebody else I know."

Cameron made a face at his brother. "Very funny."

"I don't know, Cam," Drake said. "It seems like there's a lot more to this thing with you and Shelby than you're letting on. Or maybe that you even know. Sitting here, listening to the tone in your voice and seeing the look on your face when you talk about her..." He grinned. "Maybe you should ask her out and see what happens."

Certain he must have misheard, Cameron echoed, "Ask her out? What? You mean like on a *date*?"

Drake nodded. "That's exactly what I mean."

"I can't do that."

"Why not?"

Cameron knew there were lots of good reasons why that was a bad idea. He started with the most obvious, since he'd just been pointing it out. "Shelby's life is kind of a train wreck right now."

"Yeah, she's got a lot going on," his brother agreed. "It's a good thing she's had you as a sounding board for all of it. But I kinda think that's all the more reason for you to ask her out. Sounds like she needs you." Before Cameron could comment on that, Drake added, "And you know, Cam, you've had a lot going on for a while, too. Us finding each other, Vanessa turning out the way she did, this whole Bedrock thing you're determined to get off the ground. Seems to me like you could use a sounding board yourself. And the way you talk about her, Shelby sounds like the kind of person who would be totally up for being that to someone. Maybe you need her, too."

Okay, so Drake had a point. Or, at least, a partial one. Maybe Shelby could use a helping hand, but he was just fine, thanks. Stretched a little thin at the moment, maybe, but he could handle everything by himself—the same way he always had. There were other reasons it wasn't good for him and Shelby to get involved the way Drake was suggesting, so he brought up the other obvious one. Even though Shelby still hadn't made her condition public to the world at large, he figured it was okay to tell his brother. Drake wasn't the type to gossip. And Shelby would be telling others soon, anyway, if she hadn't already.

"Shelby is also pregnant," he said.

His brother's eyebrows shot up to nearly his hairline at that. Then he leaned back in his chair and laughed. "Well, hell, that's something else you and I have in common," he said.

"What do you mean?"

Still smiling, Drake said, "If you'll remember, Annelise was also a single pregnant woman when I met—and fell for—her. Maybe there's a gene for that," he added with another chuckle. "You and I really do seem to be identical in more ways than just the physical."

"It's not the same," Cameron insisted.

"Isn't it?" his brother said meaningfully. "Look, I'm just saying that after hearing you talk about Shelby, it's obvious you have some really strong feelings for her. Okay, yeah, it hasn't been that long since you and Vanessa broke up—"

"It's been even less time since Shelby and her ex broke up," Cameron interjected.

"And there's that," Drake conceded. "But that's my point. If the two of you are spending so much time together and both like each other as much as it sounds like you do, it just makes me think you're both ready, maybe even eager, to dive back into a relationship. Especially since the people who dumped you were both so clearly not people you should've been with in the first place."

"But what about the distance between us?" Cameron countered. "As much as I enjoy it here in Emerald Ridge, my life is an hour away in Dallas. What's the point of starting something here if I'm going to be spending most of my time there?"

"You and Shelby don't have to rush into anything," Drake told him. "You've got all the time in the world. I'm just saying it doesn't make sense to not at least see where this thing takes the two of you. You deserve to be happy, Cam. The same way I'm happy now. Especially after everything that's happened."

Vanessa's face swam up before him again, and the words she spoke to him that night, about not being good enough for her, filled his ears. And, as if the two of them were as identical mentally as they were physically, Drake seemed to know exactly what Cameron was thinking about.

"Look, I know what you went through with Vanessa was awful," his brother said. "But frankly, you're lucky you found out what kind of person she is before you tied the knot. I know it hurt to lose her—or at least the *idea* of her—but can you imagine if all this had come out after the two of you had been married for years? Or had kids? You're way better off without her."

Cameron knew that. And he told his brother so. But that didn't make it any easier to forget all the terrible things she had said. All the awful ways she had made him feel. Yeah, that was on her. But what if, on some level, Shelby felt and thought the same way Vanessa did?

The two women had a lot in common, after all. They'd both grown up in the lap of luxury and were members of prominent Texas families. Plus, they both had public images they'd spent years cultivating and were obliged to maintain. Shelby was a former Miss Texas, for crying out loud. She'd almost been Miss America. Yeah, to a lot of people, that was archaic and old-fashioned and didn't mean much in the current cultural landscape. But it meant a lot to Shelby. And to a lot of other people, too.

Maybe, deep down, social trappings and appearances were as important to her as they'd been to Vanessa. And maybe, deep down, she would ultimately start to feel toward Cameron the same way his ex-fiancée had. They'd spoken enough at his penthouse after lunch the other day for him to know what kind of man her ex was. A tech genius whose family heritage was as impressive as Shelby's. His mother sat on the Texas Supreme Court, and his father was a petroleum engineer who ran a multimillion-dollar consulting business. His sister was a pediatric cancer specialist. Pretty damned impressive line that guy came from. No poor teenage single mothers or deadbeat fathers or abusive family members in the bunch.

"Just ask her out on a date," Drake said again. "See what happens. I never would have thought in a million years that Annelise and I would end up together. And, hell, now I'm the happiest man alive because of her and our baby."

Cameron eyed his brother steadily. He knew Drake wasn't lying about being blissfully happy. Every time he saw him with his family, the guy oozed joy from every pore. Truth be told, Cameron envied him that. He had never once come close to feeling as happy as Drake seemed to feel every day.

"Okay, fine," he finally conceded. "I'll ask Shelby out. And we'll see what happens from there."

Drake grinned and lifted his beer. "To new beginnings," he said.

Reluctantly, Cameron lifted his beer, too. He wasn't convinced this was the beginning of anything with Shelby. It really was nice being her friend. And he didn't want to risk screwing that up if a date with her blew up in their faces. On the other hand, he'd never know if he didn't try. So he touched the long neck of his beer bottle to his brother's with a soft *clink*. He couldn't quite bring himself to say the words out loud, though. Instead, he just enjoyed a long swallow of the cold brew and thought again about how pretty Shelby had looked when he told her goodbye before leaving her with her family a few days ago.

Shelby was leaving an empty, ready-to-rent storefront on Emerald Ridgc Boulevard that would be perfect for a pageant coaching business when she heard a familiar voice call out her name. Yes, she had officially taken the plunge. All her years about thinking of starting a coaching business had really coalesced this week and made her start planning seriously for it. No doubt Spud had a lot to do with that, since even being financially stable, she was going to need to bring in money from somewhere for the future. She had two lives to plan for now, including a college fund and travel fund so she and her son could go adventuring from time to time. There would be sports and arts and extracurriculars to pay for. Not to mention those pesky wardrobes kids tended to outgrow on a regular basis, so she was going to need a back-to-school fund. And she'd read that teenagers tended to eat their parents out of house and home. *Note to self: start a pizza fund, too.*

Plus, she just wanted to stay productive now that she wouldn't be competing anymore. It made sense to keep doing what she did best. If it couldn't be herself she was guiding through the pageant system anymore, she could help a lot of others follow their dreams. Her plans were still in their infancy at this point, but finding office space was a huge leap forward. And this one would be perfect.

At the sound of her name, she looked up to see Cameron walking toward her, his hand lifted in greeting, and she was immediately swept back to the day they met on this very street… Wow, had that been just a week ago? She honestly felt as though she'd known him her whole life. He looked every bit as handsome today as he had then, in charcoal jeans and a dark blue jacket over a crisp white shirt, a different Stetson—this one slate gray—tugged low over his forehead. Before she could stop it, the Chicks song she'd told him about over lunch the other day began to play in her head. *Cowboy, take me away...*

Immediately, she halted the tune before it could get to the *set me free* and *closer to you* parts. That way lay madness. Because she'd thought a lot about Cameron since they parted ways at her house a few days ago, when he'd left her to bask in the good news of her pregnancy with her family. Mostly, she'd thought about how he should have stayed and been a part of that basking with them. Because for some reason, Cameron Waite had felt like family, too, that day. He'd been more than a support system when she gave her mother and sister the news. And he'd been more than a friend. He'd been sweet and kind and affectionate, the way a baby's father should be at a time like that. The way Spud's father should have been. And he'd made her feel safe. Which was something else Dylan had never been able to do.

Cameron came to a halt in front of her with a smile on his face she knew must mirror her own. "Hi there," she said a little breathlessly, wondering how she could be short of breath when she was just standing on the sidewalk.

"Once again, we meet on Emerald Ridge Boulevard," he told her.

"I promise I had some lunch a little while ago so I shouldn't be fainting on you this time."

His smile broadened. "Whenever you fall, Shelby Fortune, I will always be there to catch you."

She knew he was joking. He'd said himself the other day that he might not even be in town much longer. But for some reason, instead of sharing a laugh over the comment, it seemed to make both of them feel a little flustered. Their gazes suddenly ricocheted off each other and onto everything around them that wasn't them.

Cameron pointed at the building behind her and hurried on, "What's with the empty storefront?"

Shelby turned around to look at the bright limestone-ensconced space, too. She had already started imagining the big picture window filled with pageant gowns and regalia. She could bring some of her own sashes, tiaras and gowns from home to fill it, and the sun would hit just perfectly in the afternoon to make everything sparkle like diamonds. It was going to be gorgeous. And it was going to be *hers*. She was even bandying about names for her new business. So far, People of Substance was in the lead. She would coach young people—men and women both who wanted to compete in whatever kinds of pageants were out there—to embrace integrity and purpose when they were competing for whatever titles they chose to pursue.

She turned back to Cameron and lifted the key the leasing agent had given her to let herself in. "I'm on my way back to the rental office to sign a lease for it," she told him. "It's going to be perfect for the coaching business I've thought about starting for a while now and am finally going through with."

She'd mentioned her post-pageant career plans over lunch that day at his penthouse, but now she went into more detail, about how instead of focusing on poise, dresses and the perfect cat eyeliner, she wanted to concentrate on character, personal accomplishments and community service. Sure, there would be eyeliner and outfit stuff in there, too, but she wanted to give equal emphasis to the whole person—not let physical appearance and image take center stage. Bottom line? She aimed to start a trend on the pageant circuit. One that would nip in the bud the gimmicky, on-the-spot judgments designed to go viral online before contestants even had a chance to blossom.

Cameron smiled at her announcement. "So you're really gonna do it, huh?"

She nodded emphatically. "Yes. And this space will be perfect for it. I can hire an assistant to help out part-time, and I can bring Spud to work with me until he's old enough to start school. And even then, he can come here after classes are over for the day and do his homework while I finish up."

"Sounds like you're making some pretty major plans there."

"It's definitely still a work in progress, but yeah. I have a lot of ideas percolating." She gestured down the avenue. "You want to walk with me back to the rental office? It's not far." Then she remembered something. "Oh, wait. You were probably on your way somewhere, weren't you? Don't let me keep you from whatever it was."

Cameron shook his head. "I'm not in any hurry to be anywhere." He hesitated, seeming to give great thought to something, as if he were weighing some major life decision. He opened his mouth to say more, but whatever it was was halted by the sound of another familiar voice calling out Shelby's name. It belonged to her second-grade teacher, Mrs. Shoemaker, who stopped to say hello and congratulate Shelby on her "blessed event." It wasn't the first time someone had mentioned her pregnancy. She'd been fielding congratulations and pregnancy and parenting advice for days. She was sure it was her mother who had set the grapevine into motion—probably within hours of Shelby's announcement the other day—but once those gears started turning, it hadn't taken long for what seemed like the whole of Emerald Ridge to hear the news.

So far, Shelby had been met with nothing but kindness and genuine good wishes about it. Okay, there had been one or two familiar faces who, the minute they saw her, quickly turned around and headed in the other direction. She supposed there would always be people—

no matter where you went in the world—who would be casting stones when they were worthy of a good pelting themselves. Shelby had already decided that anyone who couldn't be as overjoyed as she was about her baby wasn't of any importance to her. Spud was going to know nothing but love and acceptance wherever he went. Those who couldn't offer that had no place in her thoughts or life.

Mrs. Shoemaker gave her a hug and bid her farewell, then hurried on her way. Shelby turned to Cameron once again to find him grinning, having obviously just enjoyed the exchange between the two women as much as Shelby had.

"Cat's out of the bag about Spud, huh?" he said. "Guess it doesn't take long for news to travel in Emerald Ridge."

"You got that right. And yes, thanks to my mother, I'm pretty sure everyone in this town who's ever met me knows I'm going to have a baby. And probably plenty who haven't know that, too."

"And how are you doing with it?" he asked, sounding genuinely concerned.

"I'm good," she said, surprised to discover how very good she was just then. Of course, Cameron's appearance might have a little something to do with that. He looked awfully yummy standing out here in the brilliant afternoon that had become even more brilliant the minute she saw him. It had only been a few days since she'd seen him, but it felt more like months now that she was encountering him again. She was surprised to realize how much she'd missed him in that time. The day just suddenly felt so much…better…with him in it.

"So far, everyone's been really positive about the news," she told him. "My old piano teacher even made me promise to sign Spud up for lessons as soon as his small motor skills kick in, and Coach Salazar made it a point to tell me he can start Tee Ball League when he's four."

"Good that people are being supportive."

"Yeah." She expelled a quick sigh. "Though there's been some curiosity about Dylan and when he and I are going to tie the knot. The part about him taking off and never coming back has been a little harder to explain."

"Hopefully no one's giving you a hard time about it."

She shook her head. "No. In fact, a lot of people didn't really seem all that surprised to hear it, which I found kind of odd, then realized was pretty telling."

Cameron lifted a shoulder and let it drop. "Sometimes other people see pretty clearly the things that we don't see ourselves," he said. "My brother and I were talking about the same thing the other night."

"And how is Drake?" Shelby asked.

"He's good, too. Chatty as always. In fact, he—"

He stopped speaking abruptly, and that look came back over him she'd seen before Mrs. Shoemaker's appearance, where he seemed to be thinking about something really hard.

For a moment, he only eyed Shelby resolutely. Then he said, "Okay, I'm just going to come right out and ask."

Shelby felt a moment of alarm. "Ask what?"

His serious expression cleared some, but he was still obviously ill at ease. "Shelby Fortune, would you like to have dinner with me tomorrow night?"

Somehow, she kept her jaw from dropping to the ground. Her lips did part fractionally in her surprise, though. Certain she was misunderstanding, she replied, "What? You mean like on a date?"

He smiled, looking a teeny bit more relaxed, then nodded. "That's exactly what I mean."

She told herself she shouldn't be surprised by the invitation. She and Cameron had been getting on like a house on fire since the moment they met. Though maybe a comparison that didn't use words like *fire* would be a little better, considering the heat she was feeling at the moment. And not just because of the question, but because of how close and handsome Cameron was and how he smelled like a mix of rawhide and woodsmoke. And how she was starting to think the same kind of thoughts she'd had in the kitchen that day, then again at the restaurant that night, about—

Um, anyway, she kind of wondered why it hadn't occurred to *her* by now to ask *him* out.

Then she remembered it was because it just wasn't a good idea. Talk about *It's complicated.* Her life right now was as chaotic as a clown car. She'd just cut ties with a man she'd been certain she loved and who she'd been just as certain loved her back. Though she did seem to be getting over Dylan awfully quickly and had barely spared him a thought since he left. So yes, he obviously hadn't loved her, but it was becoming pretty evident that she hadn't loved him, either. Not in a forever-after kind of way.

Which was something else to consider. Sure, what she'd begun to feel for Cameron went beyond a friendly affection. But after everything she'd been through, could she trust her feelings for him, especially after such a short time? And her pregnancy hormones were *raging.* What if her feelings for him were the result of a hormonal change that could fluctuate wildly over the next several months?

And he could be going back to Dallas, an hour away, at any time. His whole family business—his whole life—was there. And Shelby was determined to raise Spud here in Emerald Ridge, where she'd grown up herself, because they would be close to family, and it was the perfect place to raise a child. Could she and Cameron even manage a long-distance relationship? Was it even worth trying?

Then again, how was she going to know the answer to any of those questions if she didn't give herself a chance to explore them?

She knew only a couple of seconds passed as those thoughts tumbled in her head, but Cameron was looking at her as if he'd asked her out hours ago. So she stopped thinking for a moment and let her heart decide.

"I'd love to have dinner with you tomorrow night," she told him.

He looked as if a giant boulder rolled off his shoulders at her reply. "Great," he said. "How does Italian sound? We could hit Cucina at the Emerald Ridge Hotel."

Italian sounded delicious, Shelby thought. And Cucina was one of the town's most popular date spots. If Cameron was suggesting that, then this really was going to be—

"Wonderful," she told him. "It all sounds wonderful."

He grinned again, and she did her best not to swoon. "Then I'll pick you up at your place at seven tomorrow evening."

Chapter Ten

Cameron hadn't been to Cucina during his time in Emerald Ridge, but he'd heard a lot of people talk about how good the food was and how much they enjoyed dining here. None of them, though, had mentioned just how romantic a spot it was with its gleaming granite-and-copper accents and wide windows looking out onto a lush green courtyard beyond.

Not that romantic was a problem, he thought as he followed Shelby and the hostess to their table. He'd meant it when he told her this was a *date* date, the same way Drake had suggested it be. He guessed he just hadn't really thought that far ahead. The romance part, he meant. He'd accepted that whatever had been happening between him and Shelby for the last week went beyond friendship, and the more he'd thought about Drake's suggestion that the two of them explore that with an actual night out to figure out just what they were feeling in depth, the more he'd liked the idea of asking her out. He just hadn't quite moved past what would happen after she said yes.

Now here they were, sitting down at a quiet corner table bathed in golden light and soft Italian guitar music, surrounded by the murmur of a lot of other couples who looked to be in various stages of romantic entanglements themselves. And he suddenly realized it had been a long time since he'd been out on a date with anyone besides Vanessa. Cameron hadn't dated anyone since they broke up. He hadn't wanted to. Not even any kind of superficial, getting-to-know-you-better kind of meeting in a coffee shop or bar. He hadn't met any women he wanted to get to know better. Not until Shelby. And now that they were on an honest-to-God date, he realized it wasn't even necessary to do the getting-to-know-you-better thing tonight, because he already felt like he knew her really well. Hell, he'd felt that way the day he met her. Tonight would just be…

Well. That was where his thoughts got a little blurry. Guess they'd both find out soon enough.

"I love this place," Shelby said after the hostess left them to themselves.

"Guess you've been here a lot, huh?" Cameron asked.

"Actually, it's been a while," she replied. "I think the last time I was here was…" Her eyes widened when she seemed to remember. "When Mama brought me and Jillian here to celebrate my Junior Miss Texas win. I was eighteen. Wow. Time passes fast."

That surprised him. "Didn't your boyfriends ever bring you here?"

She laughed at that. "Not since prom night. And that was a whole group of us. And it's not likc I'vc had a slew of boyfriends."

"Haven't you?"

Now she made a face. "Of course not. I never had much time for them. Plus, when you're in the pageant circuit, there's always a bit of a microscope on every aspect of your life—your family, your friends, your boyfriends.

Not a lot of guys want to deal with that. Which was always fine," she hurried to add. "Guys—relationships—were never a big deal for me. Not the way they are for a lot of people."

"What about Dylan? Didn't you and he ever come here?"

She shook her head. "Dylan was a steak-and-potatoes guy. We always went to Lone Star Selects for special occasions. All two of them. His birthday and the day some new tech thing launched that he was all excited about."

"What about your birthday?"

"He was out of town on my birthday." Her brows knitted down. "A lot like my father, now that I think about it."

She was probably thinking about that old theory that women always married their fathers, and men always married their mothers. Which was ridiculous. Vanessa had been nothing like his mother. Neither was Shelby. Not that he was planning to marry Shelby, he hastened to remind himself. They were just spending more time together because they liked one another and wanted to see where things went. If anywhere.

He was glad, though, to see how matter-of-fact she was being about her ex. The way she spoke, it was as if the two of them had been years ago, not weeks ago. Whatever hurt she might have felt at his desertion—or might still be feeling—it clearly wasn't eating her up inside.

"So what's good on the menu?" he asked her.

She looked down at the list in front of her. "I think I had the pasta cacciatore last time. I remember it being mouthwateringly delicious."

Their server returned, and since Shelby ordered sparkling water, Cameron forwent a wine selection for a bottle of that instead. They chatted about the menu selections and what was going on in town until their server returned with their drinks, then they ordered dinner and sat back in their chairs to relax.

Unfortunately, neither of them seemed to know what to say after that. Shelby looked even more gorgeous than usual tonight, her dark blond hair piled atop her head in a loose bun, with long spiraling strands framing her face. Her dress was as golden as the light enveloping them, giving her the appearance of some kind of magical woodland creature at dusk. It struck him, not for the first time, how she was the complete antithesis of Vanessa, so colorful and spontaneous where his ex had always been so tailored and self-controlled. Maybe that was why he'd connected with Shelby as quickly as he had. She was just so… real. She didn't hide the parts of herself that others might find off-putting. Hell, there were no parts of her that were off-putting. Which was another reason why he'd been drawn to her so immediately.

"You look beautiful tonight," he told her, speaking his thoughts out loud before he even realized.

When he did realize, though, he didn't regret putting the thought out there. She did look beautiful. But then she surprised him by blushing at the compliment that must have been paid her a thousand times, as if she were hearing it for the first time. "Thank you," she said with a soft smile. "You look pretty amazing yourself."

God, he hoped so. It had taken him hours to decide on the black jeans and jacket, white shirt and bolo tie with his favorite onyx slide. Then, after digging out his black alligator cowboy boots and giving them a shine, he realized his black Stetson was still in Dallas. So he'd had to go into Emerald Ridge to buy a brand-spanking-new one.

He grinned. "What, these old things? I just threw on the first thing I pulled out of the closet."

She laughed lightly. "I bet."

After that, their conversation flowed more smoothly. They talked about things they'd never discussed before over appetizers and salads, then revisited other topics they'd already chatted about over dinner. Except this time, they went into more detail about those things. He even found himself telling her about his broken engagement to Vanessa last year, something that at first surprised her, then gradually wove itself into her own experiences with Dylan. By dessert, both of them realized how lucky they were to have dodged their respective bullets.

"I just never saw it coming with Dylan," Shelby said as she stirred cream into her decaf. "I mean, now that I've had time to think about it, I realize I totally should have seen it coming. All the signs were there. I guess you just get into a lifestyle rut, and you get used to things being a certain way."

Cameron nodded. "It was like that with me and Vanessa, too."

When he first told her about the dissolution of his engagement just before the wedding, he'd glossed over the real reason for it. Now, though, for some reason, he discovered he wanted to tell her the whole truth.

"I wasn't exactly honest with you a little while ago when I told you things didn't work out between me and Vanessa because we had our differences."

She looked surprised. "No?"

He shook his head. "She was the one who had differences. Specifically, differences from me that were way too big for her to ignore."

Before he realized how much detail he intended to go into about just how badly his relationship with his ex-fiancée deteriorated, he found himself telling Shelby everything. About what Vanessa had said about his birth parents, about his "tainted bloodline," about him not being the kind of man she could ever start a life or family with.

By the end of it, Shelby looked horrified. "I do realize there are bad people all over the world," she said softly. "But I will never, ever, understand how anyone could be cruel to another living creature. Or think that other people are beneath them. How anyone could become so… *tainted*," she said meaningfully, using Vanessa's own word against herself. "And still call themselves a human being. That's not human at all."

She sounded like she'd met a few people like that herself. Immediately, Cameron found himself wishing he could protect her from ever encountering someone like that again.

She leaned forward, reaching her hand across the table to cover his. "I know you already know this, but it bears repeating. You are so much better off without her."

Cameron waited for the anger and resentment that normally roared up inside him whenever he recalled the night Vanessa told him all the terrible things she had. Then he waited some more. But no anger so much as peeped inside him. No resentment raised its head. When he thought about his ex now, he just felt…empty. As if whatever place she'd still been dwelling in inside him was vacant now, waiting to be filled with something else instead. Good emotions this time. Positive ones. Ones that made him feel better, not worse. Hopeful, not desolate.

Oh, wait. Those feelings were already kind of in there, he realized. Maybe that cold, dark place wasn't full yet, but damned if there wasn't some warmth and light filtering in. All because of the woman sitting at the table across from him.

He smiled. "Hey, what do you say we blow this joint and take a walk up Emerald Ridge Boulevard? It's a beautiful night out there."

It was a beautiful night in here, too, he couldn't help thinking. But a walk with Shelby Fortune under the moonlight sounded pretty damn good about now.

"I'd love to," she told him. "I need to work off that tiramisu before it finds a permanent place on my thighs."

Cameron laughed at that. He'd laughed a lot with Shelby this week. Because he just felt so good when he was with her.

"C'mon," he told her as he rose to help her out of her chair. "Let's see what the rest of this evening has in store for us."

Shelby supposed she shouldn't be in any way surprised that she and Cameron found themselves back at his place not long after leaving Cucina. He lived right up the street, after all. And even if he was being nice enough tonight to skip the alcohol because she couldn't have any herself, it still seemed perfectly natural for him to invite her up for a nightcap. Which ended up being a bottle of sparkling water that he poured into two wineglasses and garnished with a slice of lime. The night was young, and she wasn't ready to go home. After settling with him on the couch and falling into quiet conversation, she wasn't sure she'd ever want to go home again. Then again, being here with Cameron kind of felt like she was right where she belonged.

"So anyway," he said, winding up a story about being Willy Loman in his senior play, "for a while after that, I thought maybe I'd want to be an actor."

"You're certainly handsome enough for it," she told him. "And it sounds like you were really good in the play."

He shrugged off the compliment. "It didn't last. Nothing I ever took an interest in really did. For a while in high school, I wanted to be an Olympic track star, too. Before that, when I was a little kid, I wanted to be everything from a veterinarian to an astronaut to a center for the Dallas Mavericks."

"Did you do camps for all those?" she asked. "Jillian and I did camps for all sorts of stuff when we were kids."

He shook his head. "I wanted to. Especially space camp. But Dad signed me up for a Star Banks Adventure gaming group that year instead."

"What's that?" Shelby asked.

"It's a game to help kids learn about personal finance. But you do it in this sort of alien, outer space environment. I had fun," he assured her in a way that was no way reassuring.

Space camp would'vc bccn morc fun, though, shc suspected.

"How about you?" he asked. "Did you always want to be a beauty queen?"

"Pageant queen," she corrected him with a smile.

He smiled back. "Right. That's what I meant. Was that always your goal?"

Shelby didn't even have to think about her reply. She'd had her life mapped out since she was five years old, when she saw her first pageant on TV and fell in love with all the glamour, the color and the absolute, well, pageantry. The women on the stage had all looked like storybook princesses and fairies, and she'd wanted desperately to be a part of it, right then and there. Her mother had made her wait until she was ten to start competing, but boy, howdy, did she realize fast that she was right where she wanted to be in that world.

"As long as I can remember," she told Cameron. "I saw my first pageant on TV before I was in first grade and fell in love on the spot. I've never once doubted this is my calling. And now that I'm setting up my coaching business I think I'm going to enjoy that even better than competing."

"I wish I'd had an experience like yours," he said. "I just never really found my thing."

"You don't like being CEO of Waite Financial?" she asked, raising her eyebrows.

"It's not that I don't like it," he told her. "It's fine. And I'm good at it. But it was always kind of predetermined for me, you know? My folks—especially my dad, but my mom, too—just always assumed I'd take over when he retired. They never really encouraged me to do anything else. Every time I thought I was finding myself in some new interest or activity, they'd steer me back to the things I'd need to know to become a financier."

Shelby couldn't imagine that. Both her parents had always told her and Jillian they could do and be whatever they wanted when they grew up, and they'd always been supportive of whatever new experiences they wanted to try. Piano lessons? Sure. Rodeo camp? Why not? Renaissance dance school? Have at it.

"You could've done it anyway," she said. "Mama wasn't all that thrilled about me competing in pageants at first. But when she saw how much I loved it, she was totally on board."

"Yeah, well, even when my parents knew I loved something, they insisted I was more suited to other things. They were polite about it, but their position was always clear. Waite Financial was my destiny." He laughed, but there was no good humor in the sound. "I admit there were times in my childhood when I actually thought they'd send me back to the adoption agency if I didn't do what they wanted me to do."

Shelby's mouth dropped open. "How can you laugh about that? That's a terrible way for a child to feel. How could they have made you feel that way?"

"It wasn't them," he was quick to defend them. "It was me."

The hell it was, Shelby thought. Little kids didn't come up with those things on their own. They only felt them when the grown-ups around them made them feel that way. She took back what she said that day about his father sounding like a good guy. A good guy would never have allowed his son to think he'd send him away if he didn't do what was expected of him. He would never make his son feel like his love was conditional on whether or not he toed the line. Neither would a good mother. Automatically, Shelby opened her hand over her baby bump, and she thought about Spud. If anyone ever tried to make her little boy feel bad about liking whatever he wanted to like, she would give them a huge piece of her mind and good kick in the shin. How dare they?

She started to tell Cameron his parents had been jerks, but it took her a minute to figure out how to say that tactfully. He obviously didn't see them that way and wouldn't accept her assessment of them as such. But he started talking again before she could put her thoughts into words.

"They only wanted what was best for me," he said. "They knew me better than I knew myself."

Sounded more to Shelby like they'd only wanted what was best for them and didn't know their son at all. "If that's the case," she said, "then how come you're spending so much more time with Bedrock than you are with Waite Financial lately? Maybe you are finding your calling now. Maybe working in the nonprofit sector is more your style than working in the corporate world."

Cameron snapped his head to look at her so fast, Shelby thought it might just keep spinning around. For one tiny, infinitesimal second, he looked like he was about to realize something he'd never realized before. Then, just as quickly, the look was gone.

"The reason I started Bedrock was to honor my birth mother," he told her adamantly. "It's just taking a while to get it all organized—that's why I've had to be here in Emerald Ridge for so long. I'll be back at Waite Financial once Bedrock is under control and I can find the right people to run it."

She opened her mouth to suggest maybe *he* was the right people to do that, but he pointed to her glass. "You want a refill?"

Before she could answer, he was taking her empty glass along with his own to the kitchen. She stood up to follow, not wanting to end this conversation just when things were getting good. But Cameron must not have realized she had followed him, because after setting the glasses on the counter, he spun around to head for the fridge and nearly ran right over her. He caught her deftly, though, cupping a hand over each of her shoulders to set her to rights. Instead of stepping backward to steady herself, Shelby moved forward, bringing her body flush with his, and hooked her own hands onto his waist. She was close enough to see how the bright blue of his irises were surrounded by another ring of darker blue, close enough to smell his clean, musky scent, to feel the heat of his body mingling with hers. Close enough that, if she wanted, she could push up onto her tiptoes and kiss him.

And Shelby wanted. Oh, how she wanted. Evidently, Cameron did, too, because as she rose up and tipped back her head, he lowered his to cover her mouth with his own. And then Shelby stopped noticing anything except how he made her feel—something she'd never felt before and never wanted to let go of. Cameron made her feel *so* good. As if her entire body was silk and feathers and rose petals and he was about to wrap himself up in all of them.

For long moments, they only stood in the kitchen, their arms draped around each other, their lips brushing and skimming and caressing. Somehow, Shelby managed to pull her mouth from his, but she only moved her head far enough to look at him.

"So," she began quietly, "you said when you asked me out that this date was supposed to help us see where this thing between us might be going."

He nodded slowly. “I do remember saying that, yes.”

“Well, I’m kind of thinking maybe it should take us out of the kitchen. And then into your bedroom. What do you think?”

Only when she said it did she realize how much she had been hoping the evening would end with the two of them making love. But now that she thought more about it… Oh, yes. That was exactly where the two of them needed to be.

Cameron hesitated only a moment. “Is that what you want?”

She nodded. “Yes. I want that very much.”

He flashed a wicked grin. “Wow, that is so convenient. Because that’s what I want, too.”

She kissed him again, intertwining her fingers with his before taking a couple of steps backward—out of the kitchen, toward his bedroom. He moved right along with her, his lips never leaving hers. Shelby took a few more steps, and once again, Cameron followed. But she stopped when they were halfway across the living room and drew her head back again.

“Having second thoughts?” he murmured, his voice threaded with disappointment.

Now she shook her head. “Not for a second. But I don’t know where your bedroom is.”

Cameron turned them so that he was now backing in the same direction she had been. “Follow me.”

Step by step, kiss by kiss, they made their way down the hall—their gazes never breaking, their stride never slowing, their conviction never wavering. When they reached the bedroom, there was a single lamp burning in the corner, casting a soft, golden glow over furnishings and decor that were as lovely and generic as Cameron's public rooms were. A boxy king-size bed, nightstand and dresser, everything earthy and neutral. Somehow, though, entering the room, Shelby suddenly felt as if she'd stumbled into the most beautiful, most exciting place on the planet. When she turned to look at him, she realized he was the reason for that, of course. Everything about the man was exhilarating.

Then he pulled her back into his arms, covering her mouth with his, kissing her long and hard and deep. She tangled her fingers in his hair and kissed him back, loving the feel of the silky tresses beneath her fingertips and the soft scrape of his skin when she dropped her hand to his jaw. Loving even more the sensation of his hands on her as he caressed her back, her hips, her bottom. She itched to explore him that way, too, splaying her other hand open over his back, grazing it across the broad expanse and down to his tapered waist, then up again, over the bumps of muscle in his shoulders and arms, finally cupping his nape.

When he reached for the zipper of her dress and began to drag it downward, she fumbled for the buttons of his shirt and pants, tugging his zipper down, too. Soon, all those garments were discarded in a pile near their feet. It wasn't long before his boxers and her bra and panties joined them, and for the first time, each had unlimited access to the other. Cameron might work his jobs more than most people did, but he definitely took time to work out. His naked body was a symphony of muscle and sinew, from salient deltoids to elegant biceps to magnificent abs to mouthwatering everything else beyond. Unable to help herself, Shelby ran her fingertips over every hot, solid inch of his torso, thinking that if she could spend the rest of her life touching this man, she would die a happy woman.

Cameron took advantage of their nudity, too, lifting a hand to Shelby's collarbones, stroking first one, then the other, with the tips of his fingers. Then he moved his hand between them to skim it down her sternum between her breasts. Then lower still, to her softly swollen belly, opening his hand over her there.

"I can't believe there's a little human in there," he said softly.

Shelby covered his hand with her own. "I know. I still haven't felt him move, but he's in there, growing bigger every day."

"Pretty amazing, the whole birth thing."

"It is," she agreed.

He looked up again, his gaze meeting hers. "You're pretty amazing, too," he told her.

She smiled. "And you are quite a remarkable man."

When she leaned in to kiss him again, he moved his hand upward once more, curving first one hand, then the other, under the lower swells of her breasts. Her blood surged through her veins at the touch. Shelby knew her breasts had become more sensitive than usual during her pregnancy—even a soft touch like his brought her nearly to orgasm—and she couldn't halt the erotic sound that escaped her.

"You are so beautiful," he murmured as he closed his hands more resolutely over her tender flesh. He thumbed her nipples softly with his thumbs, and she cried out quietly again.

"So incredibly beautiful," he repeated as he backed her toward the bed.

Somehow, Shelby managed to whisper, "You're not so bad yourself."

They kissed yet again, somehow turning down one side of the bed without breaking contact. Then Cameron dropped to the edge and pulled her into his lap, straddling him, moving his mouth to her breast to pull her deeply into his mouth. Shelby cried out at the pressure of his lips and the caress of his tongue, driving her hands to his nape and her fingers into his hair again, riding out wave after wave of sensation. And when he moved his hand between her legs and furrowed his fingers into the damp, heated core of her, inserting one long finger deep inside her, she…

Oh, oh, *oh*. Shudders of an orgasm rocked through her, until she could barely remember where she was.

Eventually she realized she was side by side with Cameron on the bed, their bodies pressed together as he buried his head in her neck, her shoulder, between her breasts. As he sucked her inside again, she pushed her hand between them to find his hard, heavy shaft, gasping at his powerful length before palming the damp head. Now Cameron was the one to roar in response, pulling back long enough to look first at her face, then down at the fingers she had wrapped so possessively around him. Still watching her hand on him, he nodded once. So Shelby moved her fingers slowly from the tip to the base. He tensed when she did, and uttered another feral sound, so she snugged her fingers tighter and slowly brought them back up. Again and again, she pleasured him that way as he watched, until he suddenly wrapped strong fingers around her wrist and halted her motions.

"I want to be inside you," he said roughly.

"That's good," she whispered. "I want you inside me, too."

Cameron smiled.

Rolling her onto her back, he moved himself between her legs and began kissing and touching her again, all over. Then he was bracing his arms on each side of her, entering her as deeply as he could, and she was curling her legs around his waist to pull him in deeper still. Over and over, he drove himself inside her, then turned their bodies so that she was on top, plunging down on him, again and again, until they both cried out as one at their completion. Then they tumbled back onto the mattress beside each other, clinging to each other, breathing as if neither would ever have enough oxygen again.

For a long moment, they only gazed at each other in awe. Shelby traced Cameron's strong forehead with light fingers as he brushed his curled knuckles along her cheek. His eyes were so blue, so beautiful…and so full of an emotion she was afraid to think might be real. An emotion that was welling up inside her, too. One that may have been growing for a while. Maybe even since that first morning they met. One that nearly overwhelmed her in that moment.

Before she could stop herself, she said, very softly, "Cameron Waite, I think I might be falling in love with you."

For a moment, she didn't think he'd heard her, because he reacted not at all. Or maybe she'd only thought the words in her head and hadn't said them out loud. So she opened her mouth to try again.

She never had the chance, though. Because he suddenly tore himself away from her and jumped out of bed to immediately start gathering up the clothes they had scattered on the floor. Shelby was so startled by his abrupt withdrawal that she could only prop herself up on one elbow and silently watch as he hastily, jerkily, got dressed. But he never looked at her once. In fact, he kept his back solidly toward her.

"You know what?" he said over his shoulder. "This probably shouldn't have happened. I'm really sorry, Shelby. But I think you need to go."

He might as well have just smacked her with a wet fish—she was that stunned by the words. "I'm sorry, what?" she said in a strangled voice.

"You need to go," he repeated.

"No, I heard what you said. What I meant was what are you talking about? We were just—"

"Making a mistake," he interrupted. "That was what we were doing."

"But—"

"I mean, yeah, it was a nice mistake, for a few minutes, but—"

"A few minutes?" she echoed incredulously. "In case you didn't notice, we've been in here for more than an—"

"Okay, it was a nice mistake for longer than a few minutes," he bit out. "But it was still a mistake."

Shelby was certain she must have fallen asleep after they made love, and now she was having a nightmare. What the heck was going on? Why was he acting this way? They'd just enjoyed what, to her, had been the most beautiful, most amazing encounter she'd ever had with another human being. He'd even told her she was beautiful and amazing. He'd made her feel like she was the most wondrous creature in the world. Now, suddenly, it was all a mistake? What the…?

Then she remembered what she'd confessed to him. That she might be falling in love with him. Was that what was causing this bizarre reaction? He heard a few little words from someone about how they might have serious feelings for him? How they might love him? Was he really like so many men—like Dylan—after all? The minute someone made them feel as if they might have to include another person in their life, they turned heel and ran? Was that how he felt about her? She was fun to have *as a friend*—with benefits, obviously—while he was in Emerald Ridge, but anything more than that would be overstepping? That he didn't *want* the love she'd only said she *might* be feeling?

How could she have been so wrong about him?

She shook her head in disbelief. "Cameron, what's going on?"

Instead of answering her, though, he bent to retrieve her clothes, too, then laid them carefully on the bed, still not looking at her. "I'll give you some privacy," he said. "But really, Shelby, I think you need to go home now."

And then he was turning his back on her and heading for the door. Shelby sat up and stared at it for a long time, thinking he would come running back through it to… What? Apologize? Like an apology would even cover that? To tell her it was all a joke? Which would be the cruelest thing he could do?

What in the world had just happened? It was all she could do to get up from his bed and get dressed, willing herself not to cry when all she wanted to do was burst into tears. She could do that when she got home, she told herself. And then she could try to figure out when, exactly, she should have realized that Cameron Waite was just a jerk like the rest of the men out there.

When she exited the bedroom, she thought she was alone, because the place was as silent as a tomb, and she didn't see him anywhere. As she approached the front door, though, she finally glimpsed him, standing in the farthest corner of the living room, gazing out the window, a drink in his hand. She thought he would at least turn around and say goodbye. She even unbuckled and rebuckled her handbag when she picked it up from the foyer table, to make enough noise for him to realize she was there. But he never moved. Never spoke. Never even looked at her.

"If you want to talk," she forced herself to say, "you know where to find me." She wasn't sure why she said it. She was pretty steaming mad right now. But she wasn't ready to give up on him the way he obviously had on her.

He remained silent, though, gazing out at a dark, eerie Emerald Ridge on the other side of the window. She took a few more steps toward the front door, until she was able to curve her hand over the knob. She told herself to just leave without saying another word, but she couldn't quite make herself do it. Slowly, she pivoted around one more time.

"Because I don't think this has been a mistake at all, Cameron," she told him. She did turn the knob after that and opened the door. "Not yet, anyway."

She thought maybe she heard the ice shift in his glass

as she strode through the door, that maybe he had turned around to say something to her after all. But she must have imagined that. Either way, the damage was done for tonight.

And she had no idea if either of them would ever be able to repair it.

Chapter Eleven

When Jillian asked Shelby if she wanted to do lunch two weeks after her disastrous date—and breakup—with Cameron, she thought her sister was only doing it to try to cheer her up. It was no secret at the Fortune home that Shelby was no closer now to feeling better about the debacle of that night than she had been when it happened. Jillian had come down to the kitchen for her coffee the morning after only to find Shelby sitting at the breakfast bar in tears, where she'd been sitting since she came home a few hours earlier. Agatha had found both girls a short time later commiserating over Cameron's fierce and unexpected rejection and had joined in the sympathy fest. No amount of talking about it, though, had helped Shelby understand how things had gone so bad so quickly.

Truth be told, she still couldn't make sense of what happened that night. She'd gone back and forth between calling, or even texting, Cameron to see if they could talk and work things out and maybe try again. Ultimately, though, she'd decided it was up to him to make the first move, since he was the one who had withdrawn so completely. In an effort to facilitate that, she'd even gone into town almost daily, to stroll along Emerald Ridge Boulevard, hoping to run into him, since that had been their habit the first week they met.

But in the two weeks since that night, Cameron hadn't made any moves at all, and he'd been nowhere to be found in Emerald Ridge. She'd found that curious until she dropped into Lone Star Little Ones one afternoon, only to have Flora mention he'd had to go back to Dallas to see to some obligations at Waite Financial and she had no idea when he would be back. She said Cameron told her it could be some time before he was able to return to anything hands-on with Bedrock, and in the meantime, one of the regional people he had in place would be taking care of things. Shelby had been forced to realize then that he'd decided that Dallas, not Emerald Ridge, was where he needed—and maybe even wanted—to be.

So yeah. Looked like Cameron was well and truly gone—from town and from Shelby's life both. And whatever the something was between them that they'd wanted to explore that night—and there had definitely been *something* sparking between them—was over before it could even begin.

When she and Jillian arrived at Texas Teacups tearoom, however, she realized this outing was going to be about more than cheering her up, because Madeline Fortune was waiting for them by the door. Funny, though, how seeing her half sister waiting for them, Shelby did cheer up. She realized she'd actually missed both Madeline and Hayes since their last encounter. The half siblings had shared a handful of texts and emails since then, but they'd not made any progress in locating Lianna Dunhill or the potential missing heir.

"I figured it's been a while since we Fortune kids had a

chance to talk in person," Jillian said as they approached their newfound sibling. "So I invited Madeline and Hayes to join us for lunch. But Hayes texted that he's back in Houston talking to Penn again. I can't believe that guy still hasn't made it to Emerald Ridge. Crossing fingers that he brings our brother back this time so we can really get down to business on the Lianna Dunhill stuff."

Our brother, Shelby repeated to herself, remarking on how easily the words had fallen from Jillian's lips. They were words she never would have thought either of them would ever speak. But it was already starting to feel natural and normal—to Jillian, too, obviously—that the two of them had a much bigger family than they'd realized. A family that was kind of starting to feel like, well, family.

Jillian added, "Anyway, I also figured since it was going to be just us girls for lunch, the tearoom would be fun."

Madeline greeted them with a smile and half wave as they drew nearer, then all three women stood around a little awkwardly. Shelby couldn't help thinking how sisters, when meeting like this, would normally launch into laughing and hugging and complimenting each other's cute dresses and shoes and handbags, then tell each other what a great deal they got on everything. The Fortune sisters, however, just kind of looked at each other as if they had no idea what to say.

Finally, Madeline gestured toward Shelby's outfit and said, "Cute dress. Blue is a great color for you." About Jillian's lavender cashmere sweater set and gray trousers, she added, "Are those Amberleaf? I love their stuff."

"They are," Jillian confirmed with a smile. Then she told their half sister, "Your handbag is adorable."

"Radley of London," Madeline said, holding up the leather flower-spattered purse whose colors and pattern perfectly complemented the skirt she'd paired with a crisp white blouse. "I got it for an absolute steal."

Okay, so maybe they were becoming sisters, Shelby conceded as she watched the exchange. Texas sisters at that.

"I haven't been to this tearoom in years," Shelby said as Jillian opened the door and preceded them inside. "Mama and our au pair used to bring us here when we were kids," she told Madeline. "I always thought it was so enchanting."

It still was, she noted when they entered the tearoom proper. The proprietors had somehow managed to meld British tradition with folksy homeyness so that the whole place was filled with bright colors and whimsical accents, from the butter yellow walls filled with impressionist-type paintings of Texas wildflowers to the throw pillows embroidered with cowboy boots and horseshoes. Kind of a Queen Victoria meets Willie Nelson vibe.

"Hasn't changed a bit," Jillian agreed. "Looks just like it did when we had Shelby's birthday party here when she was, what? Five?"

"Yep. I remember how Mama tried to teach us how to pour tea like little ladies, and instead, we ended up having a scone fight with another birthday party group at the next table."

Shelby laughed at the memory. She couldn't wait to make some like that with little Spud.

Funnily, although Jillian had said the three of them could use this lunch to get each other up to speed with what they'd learned about Lianna Dunhill over the last couple of weeks—if anything—they ended up talking about themselves instead, sharing other childhood memories and remembrances of their father. What was striking, though, was how so few of their childhood memories did include their father, and how their memories of him instead seemed to mostly consist of Archibald *not* being there.

For as much as their father had insisted he loved them, he sure hadn't gone out of his way to be there for any of them. Of course, when a man had three families and a billion-dollar company to run, it wasn't surprising that he wouldn't be around much.

"I just wish he was here right now," Madeline said softly, "so we could ask him why he did all the things he did and whether or not he truly loved any of us."

Jillian nodded. "Like Shelby said before, maybe he really did crave love so much that he surrounded himself with people to love who would love him back. But then maybe loving all of them made him realize how much he had to lose, and that scared him so badly that he had to back away from everyone."

Shelby almost heard a little *ding* in the back of her brain at her sister's words. They made so much sense. A man who had never known what it was like to be loved by anyone could be paralyzed by the feeling when he finally experienced it because he'd had no idea how powerful it could be. It was scary to love someone with all your heart. What if something bad happened to them or you lost them? And people who loved you knew all your weaknesses and insecurities. You were vulnerable to them and had to trust them not hurt you. That was a scary thing to do. It could be downright terrifying to hand yourself over to another person, lock, stock and barrel.

But most people pushed past that fear, because the reward of loving someone—and being loved in return—was life's greatest joy. But for people who'd never known genuine love because they'd never been given it…

She thought about Cameron and remembered the things he told her during their solitary date before everything had gone so wrong. About how his ex-fiancée had used his background and identity to make him feel small and tell him he wasn't good enough. About how his parents had never seemed to want to see the real him when he was a child. How their love had felt conditional while he was growing up. It must have hurt like hell to hear people he loved—people he trusted to never, ever hurt him—say things that cut him to his core.

In a lot of ways, she suddenly realized, Cameron was like her father. Not in the neglectful, absent ways—on the contrary, he was the most considerate, present-in-the-moment person she'd ever met. But in the scared-little-boy ways. All the people he'd loved, who had told him they loved him back, had either made that love provisional or eventually taken it back. Essentially leaving him alone. No wonder he'd reacted the way he had when Shelby told him she was falling in love with him. The little boy inside him had roared up and become terrified she would hurt him and take it away, too.

Wow. Nothing like having a major epiphany in the middle of Texas Teacups. Now she just had to figure out how to help Cameron have one, too.

Jillian and Madeline were still chatting amiably, as if Shelby had just stepped out to go to the powder room, and it took her a minute to get caught up. Madeline was talking about the event-planning business she wanted to open called Let's Get This Party Started, and how she was finding Emerald Ridge such a nice place that she was seriously thinking of opening it right here and hanging around.

"You'd certainly get a lot of business," Jillian said. "I don't think we have anything like that in Emerald Ridge right now."

Shelby nodded. "And it seems like every time I turn around these days, someone has some kind of celebration or party going on. Not just birthdays, but weddings, engagements, baby showers, you name it."

"Actually," Madeline said, "it's interesting you mention birthdays, because the day after I got here in Emerald Ridge, I received a call from Kate Fortune, who wants to hire me to plan her one hundredth birthday party in July. Do you two know her?"

Shelby and Jillian exchanged looks that were nothing short of awed by the woman in question. Then they started laughing.

"Are you kidding?" Shelby said. "The whole reason Daddy has Fortune Air is because of Kate. I mean, we never met her, but he told us the story when we were kids—a million times, probably—about how she loaned him the start-up money to launch his empire."

Jillian added, "Dad was a teenager with nothing, and knowing how successful she was with her cosmetics business and that they were distantly related, he finagled a meeting with her. He told Kate how he was a Fortune, too, but a poor one, and was living in barns and working hard and had a dream of starting an airline someday to take him away from it all. And he asked if she could help him out."

Madeline began smiling as they spoke. "And she was so charmed by him that she gave him a thousand dollars with the caveat that that was all he was going to get from her, so he better use it wisely. Yeah, I heard that story, too, when I was growing up. *A lot.*"

Shelby and Jillian laughed with her.

"Of course you did," Shelby said. "I'm sure Daddy told all of us about Kate whenever he could."

"Did you also know," Madeline continued, "that he sent her a card every year on the anniversary of the day he started Fortune Air to tell her thank you?"

The sisters exchanged another look, then turned back to their half sister. "We did not," Shelby said.

"I didn't, either," Madeline said. "Not until Kate told me that in the last card she received from him, he wrote that if she was planning a party for her one hundredth birthday, there was no one better than his daughter Madeline to organize it."

So Archibald did think about them, Shelby thought wistfully. He had cared. Maybe it really was true that he had loved them all so much that it had kind of scared him.

Madeline sighed. "I think probably he also wanted to help me out the way Kate helped him once upon a time. He knew I was coming off of a bit of a..." She expelled a restless sound. "My career took a big hit not too long ago because of a disaster at a major party I planned for the company I used to work for. Not to mention my being sabotaged by my ex around the same time. Not only did I lose my job, but it's been next to impossible for me to find any new clients in Dallas. That's a story for another day, though," she concluded with a sad smile. "Anyway, this party for Kate is going to be a very good thing for me. It's another reason I'm thinking of opening Let's Get This Party Started here. I think it's going to be a fun event to plan, and I think it's going to lead to a lot of good things."

Shelby opened her hand over her rounded belly, even fuller now than it had been two weeks ago. "I know of a certain mom who will need your services for a first birthday party next year."

She remembered then how she'd promised Cameron he would receive an invitation to that party. Was that a promise she was going to be able to keep? Was a promise she even wanted to keep? Tearoom epiphanies aside, even if he came back to Emerald Ridge, was there a chance they could work things out after the hurtful way that night played out? She honestly wasn't sure.

"I'll put you on my calendar," Madeline told her with a chuckle, bringing her out of her morose thoughts for now. "But first things first. We need to find Lianna Dunhill."

Now Shelby was the one to sigh. "Yeah. Lianna Dunhill. A woman who seems like dust in the wind. What are we supposed to do about her?"

She suddenly felt a soft tap on her shoulder, followed by a feminine voice asking, "I'm so sorry, I don't mean to interrupt."

She turned in her chair to find two women seated at the next table, both gray-haired and grandmotherly. The one closest to her, who had tapped her on the shoulder, still had her hand raised and was smiling tentatively. "Did I just hear you girls say the name Lianna Dunhill?" she asked.

Shelby had honestly begun to think there simply was

no one who existed on the planet named Lianna Dunhill, so fruitless had their search for the woman been so far. Yet here was a total stranger who had recognized the name. Her heart rate actually jumped at the realization.

"Yes, we did," she told the woman as she turned more firmly in her seat to speak to her. "Do you know her?"

"I *knew* her," the woman replied. "She's been gone from Emerald Ridge for a long time. I was actually good friends with her aunt Jeri, who lived here. Little Lianna would visit when she was a girl, then she moved here when she was a teenager after what I believe was some trouble at home. I don't know the details. But Jeri wasn't in great health at that point. Lianna was sent to help her out."

Shelby could scarcely believe her ears. Or their good luck. Lianna Dunhill *did* exist! Even better, someone had actually seen her with their own eyes. She looked at her sisters, who seemed to be as amazed as she was. Then she turned back to her new friend.

"Does Jeri still live here?" she asked hopefully.

"I'm afraid not," the woman said. "She left town a few years after Lianna did. Her health began to deteriorate quickly, and she needed to be near someone who could take care of her."

From Shelby's other side, Jillian asked the women, "So Lianna was Jeri's caregiver when she lived here?"

Now it was the two women at the next table who exchanged a look. And judging by their expressions, neither had much regard for Lianna.

The first woman turned to Jillian. "No. She was supposed to, but she moved out of Lianna's house the day she turned eighteen to live above the restaurant where she was working. She completely ignored Jeri after that. Frankly, I don't think Lianna Dunhill ever *cared* for anyone. Except for herself." She immediately looked chastened. "I'm sorry. I shouldn't speak ill of other people."

Shelby deflated some. "Then I gather you don't know where Lianna went after she left town."

"I'm afraid not, dear. I don't even know where Jeri went. No one in Emerald Ridge does. After her health took a turn for the worse, she started keeping to herself. Then one day, her house was up for sale, and she was gone. When I heard you girls mention Lianna, I was hoping maybe *you* would be able to help *me*. I still think about Jeri from time to time. I'd love to know where she is and how she's doing."

"We didn't even know Lianna had an aunt until just now," Madeline said from the other side of the table. "We're looking for her, too. Our whole family is. We were beginning to think she didn't exist."

"Oh, she definitely existed," the woman said. "After she left town, Jeri tried to find her, but back in those days, it was impossible to locate someone who'd gone missing without the help of law enforcement. And the police told Jeri that Lianna was a grown woman who was perfectly within her rights to leave town. Unless she had some reason to believe her niece had met with foul play, there was nothing they could do."

Shelby wasn't sure how much she should say about Lianna's reasons for leaving Emerald Ridge to a stranger, so she said nothing. Neither of the women at the next table seemed to expect a reply, though. Instead, they began to gather up their things and stood to leave.

"Was Jeri's last name Dunhill, too?" Shelby asked before they could get away.

"No, it was Ward," her new friend told her.

"Maybe we can find her and see if she has any info about Lianna."

"If you do find her, dear, would you let me know? I'll give you my number, then we have to skedaddle." Her new friend scribbled her name and number on a beverage napkin and handed it to Shelby.

"I sure will," Shelby promised as she tucked it into her purse.

The two women thanked her and told all three Fortunes to enjoy the rest of their day, then they made their way to the front door. The minute Shelby turned back around, she pulled out her phone and started searching for Jeri Ward.

"Finding anything?" Jillian asked after a moment.

Shelby shook her head. "Not really. It's a common enough name—for women and men both—that too many come up."

"Try spelling it a different way than you are," Madeline said.

Shelby did. She tried spelling it several different ways, first with J's then with G's. But that didn't help much, either. She added the word *Texas* to the mix. Better, but still too many. Finally, she added *Emerald Ridge*.

"Bingo!" she finally said, looking up at her sisters.

"What have you got?" Jillian asked.

Shelby put her phone flat on the table so the others could see what she'd found. "A listing on one of those find-people sites," she told them. "Apparently there's a Jeralyn Ward who lived in Emerald Ridge at a time that coincides with Lianna being here, too."

"Looks like her residence after Emerald Ridge was Terrell," Madeline said. "That's a Dallas suburb. But she's moved a few times since then, it seems."

"And now she's in a place called Bisonville," Jillian noted. She looked up. "Anybody know where Bisonville is? I've never heard of it."

Madeline and Shelby shook their heads, then Shelby retrieved her phone and did some more searching. "Found it," she told her sisters, turning her phone so they could see the map, too.

"That's barely an hour away," Madeline said.

"And not a bad drive," Jillian added.

"Looks pretty small," Shelby noted. "Which means it shouldn't be hard to navigate once we get there."

She picked up her phone and went back to the site where she'd found Jeralyn's address. "There's a phone number listed, too," she said.

Neither Jillian nor Madeline said a word. They only looked at her as if she should know exactly what to do. And Shelby did. After thumbing the link to the number, she hit the speaker icon and held the phone between the three of them. It rang and rang and rang, then finally picked up. She was about to say hello but was met with the screechy tone that indicated the number had been disconnected, followed by a recorded voice telling them that the number was no longer in service and to please hang up and try again. She punched her phone off.

"We have to tell Hayes and Penn," she said. "When they get back, we can all drive to Bisonville to talk to Jeralyn Ward about her long-lost niece Lianna."

"I don't think it's a good idea for all of us to go," Madeline said. "If Jeri was in poor health when she left, which was a lot of years ago, who knows what's going on with her now? She might not appreciate a bunch of strangers descending on her at one time."

"Good point," Jillian said. "Maybe just Shelby and I could go, since we can talk to her about Emerald Ridge. She might actually like meeting a couple of people from the place where she grew up. What do you think, Shelby?"

"I think it's perfect. Let's go as soon as we can."

The three women let out nearly identical sighs of relief.

"Our first real clue," Jillian said.

Shelby nodded. "One that, with any luck, will lead us to at least a few answers."

It was raining in Dallas. Again. Cameron gazed out the window of his father's office in his parent's house in Highland Park, watching fat droplets streak the windows and pelt the trees outside. He'd stayed home from Waite Financial today in the hope that it would make him more productive, having fewer distractions. By working here, he'd thought, it would help him at least focus on the things at work that were most important. But every time he'd sat down to do that today, he'd found another reason to do something else instead. He'd left something in his briefcase. Then he needed to google something for Bedrock. Then he needed to top off his coffee. Then he needed to google something else for Bedrock. Then something else for Bedrock. And something else again.

Nothing at Waite Financial felt important, that was all. Not even after he'd been away from it for months. Working here in his father's office, where he'd figured the lingering ghost of his dad would spur him to get back to work, hadn't helped in any way. And all the damned rain they'd been having was just making it worse.

Hang on a minute. It wasn't raining *again*, he realized. Today's downpour was actually the first rain he'd seen the entire month of February. The weather had been sunny and clear in Dallas since he'd come back. It only felt like he'd been staring at rain and clouds for as long as he could remember.

He turned away from the window to look at the office instead. He'd tried to think of it as his office after taking over for his father at Waite Financial. But nothing in this room felt like it was his. Because nothing in this room felt like him. Nothing in this whole house felt like him, even after spending nearly his whole life here. As much as he'd tried to update his childhood bedroom and make it more grown-up, there was nothing of him in there, either. By taking down the trappings of his youth, he'd only ended up making the room soulless and sterile instead. Then again, maybe that was because, as an adult, Cameron had always felt kind of soulless and sterile, too.

Well, except for one warm, wonderful week in Emerald Ridge, with a beauty queen—excuse him, pageant queen—who'd made him feel like a king. But that week with Shelby hadn't been real life, he told himself for maybe the hundredth time since coming back to Dallas. At least, it hadn't been his life. His life was in Dallas. It always had been. Even if there was nothing here that felt real anymore, either.

He moved out of the office and into the hallway, down the stairs to the first floor, through the living room, library, and dining room, until he found himself in the kitchen. Where, yep, it was still raining. Both outside the house and inside his head. Maybe there had never been anything of him here, he thought. Again, not for the first time. In Dallas or this house. Certainly there was nothing that had made him feel as if he'd come home when he came back. Honestly, the only place and time that had ever come close to feeling like that had been that night at his condo on Emerald Ridge Boulevard, when he and Shelby had—

He halted the thought before it could form. But it formed anyway. The warmth of her skin beneath his fingertips. The softness of her mouth against his. The way he'd felt when she circled her arms around his waist and pulled him deeper inside her, as if she would never let go. As if she would never let him go. As if she would make it her life's work to ensure that he was happy and that no one would ever hurt him again.

Cameron closed his eyes and let the feelings wash over him, the way he hadn't let them that night. Because they'd been too new and too different from anything he'd ever felt. Because it had been frankly terrifying to feel so much, so deeply, for another human being.

Because it had been terrifying to fall in love with Shelby Fortune and know somehow that she would leave him, too.

And now here he was, alone the way he'd known he always would be. But that was on him, not Shelby. Because he was the one so paralyzed by fear that he'd had to withdraw completely.

He made his way back through the house and upstairs again, back to the office that looked the same way it did thirty minutes ago. Hell, thirty years ago. Nothing had changed one whit in this house during his lifetime. Nothing had changed one whit at Waite Financial, either. But he'd changed, Cameron realized now. He'd changed a lot. And, looking back, he realized it had happened pretty much overnight. He could pinpoint the moment exactly. The minute Shelby Fortune fell into his arms. All this time, he'd been thinking he was the one who'd caught her when she fell that day. But now he realized he'd been falling that day, too, even faster and harder than she had. He'd been falling for months before he met Shelby. Maybe years. Maybe his whole life. That day when he caught her on Emerald Ridge Boulevard, she'd turned around and caught him right back.

He'd been such an idiot. How could he have left her like that? Left her, hell. He'd practically thrown her away.

He bit back a frustrated growl and shook his head. Vanessa's words had really done a number on him. He'd been so wrapped up in thinking the worst about himself that night that he hadn't been able to appreciate the best thing that ever happened to him. Nah, he told himself further. It wasn't Vanessa who'd done that. It was himself. He'd let words that should have been meaningless to him outweigh feelings that should have been real. Words that were meaningless, he knew now. And feelings that were real. He knew that now, too.

He was done being haunted by the ghost of a past he should be celebrating instead. His birth mother had been a survivor. She'd been strong enough to do the right thing, even when it meant making a massive sacrifice. She'd put the people she loved—him and Drake—ahead of herself. She sure as hell hadn't let someone else's opinion of her diminish her in any way. And he'd bet good money she never once told him or Drake that they were a mistake, the way he'd told Shelby their lovemaking was.

Something hot and unpleasant rolled through his belly at the memory. He'd behaved abominably that night. Because he'd been too blind to what was happening between them. When she told him she thought she was falling in love with him, he should have told her he was falling in love with her, too. Because he'd realized in that moment that he was in love with Shelby Fortune. And it had scared the ever-loving life out of him. He was still in love with Shelby. He knew he would be in love with her until the day he died. And that still scared him. It would probably scare him till the day he died.

But what scared him more was the prospect of a life without her. And the thought that he might have screwed up so badly that he'd lost her forever.

What they'd shared that night hadn't been a mistake at all. He knew that now. Hell, that night with Shelby had probably been the first thing in his whole life that *wasn't* a mistake. It was for sure the first thing he could remember that felt right. He just wished he knew how he could tell her that. How he could explain to her that he loved her and needed her and would do whatever it took to make things work between them. How he could make her believe that he would never leave her side again. But just how was he supposed to do that after the things he said and did that night?

He looked at the clock on the wall. The workday was almost over. Not that he'd gotten any work done today. Well, none for Waite Financial at least. He'd gotten a lot of work done on himself. He knew there was still work to be done, there, too, but at least he was on his way. He could see some light at the end of the tunnel.

He smiled at the metaphor. It must be the light Shelby had turned on inside him the day they met. It had been kind of dim at first, and it hadn't done much to reveal the path he needed to get on. But now that light was starting to be quite…illuminating. He looked out the kitchen window and saw that the rain was lessening, and the thick gray clouds that had been in the sky all morning were starting to break up. If he'd ever been the kind of person who needed a sign, he knew he had it. There were a few things he needed to clear up here in Dallas before he could return to Emerald Ridge. But he would most definitely be returning to Emerald Ridge.

He just hoped Shelby was still speaking to him once he got there.

Shelby couldn't help popping into Lone Star Little Ones a couple of days after her lunch with Jillian and Madeline, just to have a quick look around. And also to give her brain something else to do than fill her head with thoughts about Cameron Waite, which it always insisted on doing whenever she didn't have something else to think about instead. What was worse was how the more time that passed after his departure from Emerald Ridge, the more vivid her memories about him became. The least her brain could do was use one of those Hollywood filter lenses or something, to make thoughts of him hazier and more distant. But *nooo*. Every place she went in town, there was something that made a memory pop into her head, as clear as the moment it happened. And every time it happened, Shelby just missed Cameron more.

She couldn't help it. He'd behaved like an absolute rat that night. He'd thrown her words of love for him back in her face as if they were poison. He'd hurt her that night. Badly. How could she miss him?

Because as often as she replayed that painful evening, she replayed even more all the other moments with him. Moments that had been anything but hurtful. Moments when he had been kind and gentle and caring. She just wished she knew what to do to find that Cameron again.

She braced herself for another memory of him as she opened the door to Lone Star Little Ones. But her attention went right to Flora, instead, who was assembling a triceratops-shaped bookcase that would go perfectly with the ankylosaurus toy box Shelby picked up last week. She bought one on the spot, wrestled it into the back seat of her car, then drove home feeling both a sense of accomplishment and relief that she'd have something to keep her mind off of Cameron for the rest of the day.

In truth, she had no idea why she'd chosen a dinosaur theme for Spud's nursery, but once it popped into her head, it just felt right. She'd grabbed a few other things with the toy chest that day and stashed them all in the large walk-in closet next to her bedroom until she knew what to do with them. Now, as she leaned the box with the bookcase against one wall, she looked around at the closet that was really more of a dressing room, complete with a small window that looked out over the rolling hills behind the house. And she got an idea. Her dressing room would be the perfect spot for Spud's nursery.

Unless, of course, they never found Lianna Dunhill or their missing sibling. Then this house could go on the chopping block and its proceeds to her father's charities instead. She knew she would land on her feet if that happened, that she and Spud would be fine no matter where that landing left them. But she couldn't stand the thought of losing her childhood home. Even if everything ultimately worked out with her missing sibling, and she and Spud wound up living in their own place someday, she wanted him to be able to enjoy the spectacle of the holidays here. She wanted him to have the same wide open spaces to run around in as a child that she'd had. It would just hurt—a lot—not to be able to call Fortune and Daughters Ranch her home.

She spent what was left of the day and the one after it getting her dressing room in shape. She went through all the clothes and accessories, separating everything into Keep and Give Away piles, then made arrangements to have her gowns and pageant paraphernalia moved to the space she'd secured in town for People of Substance. With the help of their housekeeper, Roxie, she thoroughly cleaned the shelves and cabinets, leaving those white and painting the walls with the merest hint of aqua blue. And if the color only served to remind her of Cameron's eyes, and his smile, and the wonderful way she'd felt whenever he was around, then…

Well. She'd just think about something else.

In fact, *not* thinking about Cameron made her more industrious and productive than she'd ever been in her life. Within two days of deciding the dressing room would be Spud's nursery, Shelby was sitting in its center after dinner with a toolbox open by her side and triceratops and ankylosaurus parts strewn about the floor around her. She wasn't going to go to bed until they were both whole. Even if she was already halfway there in her cartoon-cat-spattered pajamas and her hair still a damp, messy bun atop her freshly showered head.

There was a soft rap on the doorjamb, and she looked up to find her mother gazing in.

"Wow, you've come a long way on this," Agatha said.

Shelby went back to tightening a screw in a dino foot. "Yeah, who knew having someone break your heart could make you so damned productive?"

Her mother's expression turned a little pained. "You, um, have a visitor, dear."

Shelby looked up again to tell her mother she was kinda busy at the moment and really wasn't in a mood to see any—

Then Cameron poked his head around the door beside her mother.

"He's very insistent," Agatha said.

"Hey," he said softly. "Can we talk?"

Shelby looked at her mother for support. Instead, Agatha only smiled and lifted a hand to wiggle her fingers goodbye, then disappeared.

Shelby's heart leaped into her throat. Cameron was even more handsome than she remembered, his dark blond hair recently cut and his face freshly shaven, dressed in charcoal jeans and a Western-style shirt the same color as his eyes. He smiled a tiny, uncertain smile as she looked at him, as if he wasn't sure what his reception would be. Shelby didn't know yet what his reception would be, either. She was still angry and confused about his behavior the last time she saw him, and in spite of her realizations at the tearoom a few days ago, she still wasn't sure she understood any of it. She told herself to stand up and at least say hello, but sitting as she was, she knew that was going to be an awkward maneuver. Her baby bump was growing by the day, and her balance was shifting accordingly. If she tried to get to her feet now, she was going to end up looking like that scary girl coming out of the television in the *Ring* movies. So she stayed put.

As if he'd picked up on her horror-movie thoughts, Cameron said softly, "Could you at least put down the screwdriver? I know I'm not your favorite person at the moment."

What was weird was that that wasn't exactly true. Even after everything that had happened, Cameron still kind of was her favorite person. At least, the Cameron she knew before that night at his condo.

When she still didn't move, he told her, even more quietly, "I'm sorry I broke your heart."

The pieces of her heart melted a little at that. She sighed and set the screwdriver on the floor. "Fine. But I'm not getting up."

His relief that she was talking to him at all was almost palpable. He strode into the room and dropped down to sit on the floor beside her. Not super close. But not far away, either. Kind of halfway between her and the exit. The symbolism of that strangely reassured her.

"And I'm sorry about...what happened that night," he said with much understatement.

She nodded carefully. As good as it felt to see him again, it kind of hurt, too. "And what exactly *did* happen that night?"

He blew out a ragged breath. "It took me a while to figure that out myself." But he seemed hesitant to say more.

"And did you? Figure that out?"

He nodded. "I just… When you said what you did that night…"

"That I thought I was falling in love with you?" she asked pointedly, mostly because she wanted to see if he would react the same way now that he had then.

He didn't react that way at all, though. He smiled. Happily, but a little wearily, too. As if he were glad to hear her say the words again and had feared he never would.

"Yeah, that," he told her. "When you said you might be falling in love with me, I just… I panicked, Shelby."

"Why?"

Now he hesitated not at all. "Because I knew I was falling in love with you, too."

Something inside her that had been wound too tight for much too long eased, and she felt as if her entire body was freed of a very heavy weight. She said nothing, though. She only gazed at him expectantly, silently willing him to go on.

"Every time I've loved someone," he said, "they've made me feel like…" He blew out a restless sound. "I don't know. They've always loved me on their terms, not mine. I think there's always been a part of me that was afraid anyone who loved me would stop loving me if I turned out to not be what they wanted me to be. So I made myself be whatever they wanted, because I didn't want to lose them. But you, Shelby…"

He smiled now, in a way that lit up the whole room. "I've been nothing but myself with you since I met you. Because you never expected me to be anyone but myself. And you *liked* me when I was myself. That never happened before." A quiet calm seemed to wash over him.

"For the first time in my life, I didn't feel like I had to be or do something for you to accept me. You know why?"

"Why?" she asked breathlessly, clinging to his every word.

"Because it never once occurred to me to do or be anything but myself with you. You're just so open, so honest with your thoughts and feelings. You would have told me flat out if you didn't like me the way I was or if you expected me to be something else. But you only wanted me to be me. I loved that about you from day one."

Shelby wanted to reach for him and take his hand and tell him she loved him, too. But he was too far away, and he started talking again.

"But even after realizing that," he said thickly, "I think there was a part of me that thought, deep down, you would end up being like the others. That you would take off if I wasn't good enough for you."

She shook her head. "I would never think that about you, Cameron. My God, there are people in town who think *I'm* not good enough, having a baby as a single mom. And you know what? I don't give a damn what anyone thinks of me. Or my family. Or anything else, for that matter. Vanessa was the one who cared about all that crap. Not me."

"I know that now," he said. "But you and Vanessa have a lot in common, and—" He held up a hand to stop her when she was about to object to that—strenuously. "You both have public images and come from long, illustrious bloodlines, and—"

"Images are mirages," she told him. "There is literally nothing substantial to them. And bloodlines are for pumping blood through our body to keep us alive. That's it. Everybody has a bloodline, Cameron, and they all look the same under our skin. Anyone who thinks they're important for anything on the outside else are just full of hooey."

He grinned again. "See? There's that open honesty I love so much."

She smiled back. "I love you, too."

He sobered. "I don't want to lose you, Shelby. That was why I panicked that night. Because the thought of losing you was just so much worse than the thought of losing anything—or anyone—else in my life. It scared the hell out of me that night to realize that, and I… I just panicked. I didn't know what to do."

Shelby's eyes filled with tears as he spoke. He'd had the very epiphany she had hoped he would, but she hated that he'd thought she could ever, *ever*, turn her back on him.

"How could you ever think you're not good enough? That my love would ever be conditional on anything? I'm about to launch a business called People of Substance, for Pete's sake—as in what's inside, what people are truly made of. Not appearances. Not image. *Substance.* The qualities that truly make someone a good person. Like you are."

She stopped to take a steadying breath.

"I mean, yeah, you look amazing—" She smiled. "—but that's not what makes me love you. I love you for what's inside. For what makes you *you.*"

She managed to scoot close enough to him to cover his hand with hers and squeeze it tight.

"Cameron Waite, you are the best person I have ever met. And I love you more than I can ever tell you. So I guess I'll just have to spend the rest of my life showing you."

He scooted closer, too, draping his arm over her shoulder and pressing his forehead against hers. "I am so glad to hear you say that. Because I'm about to move to Emerald Ridge full-time, and I was hoping you and I could spend a whole lotta time together after I do. Like every day. Every week. Every month. And Spud with us, once he's here."

She wrapped an arm around his waist. "What about your life in Dallas?"

He gave her shoulder a soft squeeze. "I don't have a life in Dallas," he told her. "I never had one there. Not the kind I wanted…or was suited to." Now he pulled back enough to meet her gaze. "I never felt like I was a part of the world my parents raised me in. Honestly, I think on some level, I never felt like I was a part of my own family. I know my parents loved me in their way. But they didn't love me like…" He pressed a quick kiss to her temple and looked at her again. "They didn't love me like you do, Shelby."

"You mean wholeheartedly from their heads to their toes, no matter what happens until they can barely think straight?"

He grinned. "Yeah. Like that. Since coming to Emerald Ridge and meeting you, I have finally found the place where I belong, and the work I want to do. I feel so at home here with you. It took me a while to realize that, because I'd just never known what that felt like."

Her heart—whole now that the pieces had been mended—melted again. She was happy Cameron had finally found his footing. She was even happier that he'd found it here with her.

Still…

"What about Waite Financial?" she asked. It was a

generations-old business after all that had been run by Waites for a long time.

"I have a lot of plans for the company," he told her, "but none of them include me. I want to make Bedrock my focus now. I want to be its CEO, and I want to headquarter it here in Emerald Ridge. I've loved all the work I've done on it so far, and I'm good at it. And it's good work to do. My board of directors at Waite Financial has been made aware of my plans, so the gears are in motion there. There's also an auction company going through my parents' house in Dallas as we speak to clear out the things I didn't want to hold on to, and I have a Realtor lined up to list it when they're through."

She scooted the last few inches to bring their bodies as close as they could be. "Wow. Guess you'll be moving a lot of that stuff to Emerald Ridge, then."

"Not much of it, really," he told her. He gave her shoulder another squeeze and dropped his other hand to her baby bump. "Everything that's most important to me, Shelby, and everyone I love is right here."

Me, too, Shelby thought as she joined her hand with his over the life that was growing inside her. *Oh, baby. Me, too.*

* * * * *